THE SOLDIER AND THE COWBOY

VANESSA GRAY BARTAL

DRY CREEK PRESS

Maggie and Cameron Ridge sat on their couch, attempting to cuddle each other while their giant dog forcibly cuddled them, stretching overtop them and filling all available spaces.

She held a book in hand, resting on the dog's chest, and he tried to watch the game around the dog's airborne hind leg.

"We should get a cat," Maggie said suddenly. Ridge muted the television and looked at her.

"Why, exactly, would we add to this menagerie?" he asked.

"To give the dog a friend. He gets so lonely when we're at work."

"You want to get a pet for our pet?" he asked.

"Not just that. Lately I've been feeling like, and don't freak out, but maybe a tiny bit of baby fever. I have the strongest desire to cuddle something so hard." She ground her fist into her open palm.

"Hello, I'm sitting right here, your adoring husband. Cuddle me," he said.

"You don't smell right," she said.

"Ouch."

"No, I mean you smell incredible, but it's not the right smell to get rid of this feeling. I need something tiny and loaded with baby pheromones to quell my raging estrogen. It's like when The Hulk goes green, but instead of stomping around in anger destroying things he picks them up and loves on them."

"You know I don't understand it when you talk comic book. But I have a brilliant idea: instead of a cat, why don't we, I don't know, have a baby," he suggested.

"You're playing pretty fast and loose with the word 'we' there. 'We' won't have morning sickness, and 'we' won't gain thirty pounds, and 'we' won't have to push it out of 'our' body, and 'we' won't have to make difficult decisions about work when it's over."

"No, but 'we' will do the hard work of caring for it together, of picking up the slack for each other when one of us is lagging, and this half of 'we' is extremely looking forward to seeing you pregnant." He attempted to shove the dog aside to reach for her, but the dog was having none of it and instead pushed its foot into Ridge's face.

"I don't think I'm there yet, but I'm closer," Maggie said. She kissed her two fingers and reached over the dog to place them on Ridge's lips.

"If the dog has his way, we'll never procreate," Ridge complained.

"He wants to be our only baby forever," Maggie agreed. "But you will love being a big brother," she added to the dog, scratching his belly.

"I could go for some of that, too," Ridge added hopefully, and she laughed. "Laughter, great, that's what I wanted from that statement."

"You have to know how to handle the dog," Maggie informed him. "Smokey, ball." The dog jumped down and ran eagerly for his toy basket and squeaky ball. Meanwhile Maggie closed the gap between them and slid her arms around Ridge's neck. "You know, I'm not ready for a baby, but I wouldn't mind a practice session, a pre-baby-making warm up, if you will." She leaned into him, bit his ear, and he tossed aside the remote.

"No way I'm saying no to that," he said, and then the doorbell rang. They froze, debating whether or not to answer it. "Were we expecting someone?"

She shook her head. "Better answer it." In their world, surprises were usually bad news.

He stood and held up a finger. "Don't lose our place."

"Librarians are aces at bookmarking," she assured him.

He had no idea who might be calling unexpectedly, but even so he couldn't have been more surprised to see his boss standing on his doorstep. "Colonel, sir," he said, automatically standing at attention, despite having been out of the navy for a few years now.

"As you were," The Colonel said. It was probably his most oft-used phrase because he was the kind of man even civilians came to attention for.

"Come in, sir," Ridge said, stepping aside to allow him entrance.

Maggie stood when he entered the living room, but not to come to attention. Instead she stepped forward and hugged him. "Colonel, what a nice surprise. Can I get you a piece of peach pie, sir? I just pulled it out of the oven an hour ago."

"I can't resist your pie, Maggie, thank you," he said, returning her hug.

She left the room to dish the pie, and Ridge's eyes followed her with wonder. He would never get used to the fact that a man who inspired such terror in others—and rightly so—treated his wife like a long lost, much cherished daughter. "Have a seat, sir," Ridge offered, drawing his attention back to the man before him.

"Thank you," The Colonel said, taking a seat on the couch. Right away Smokey ran up to him and deposited his ball in his lap.

"Smokey," Ridge admonished.

"It's fine," The Colonel said. He picked up the slobbery ball and tossed it across the room while Smokey took off after it, nails scrambling on the floor.

"Is everything all right, sir?" Ridge asked. The Colonel had never come to his home before, and he was dressed in civilian clothes, another first.

"I, uh, have a kind of favor to ask," The Colonel said, shifting uncomfortably.

"Anything," Ridge said and meant it. He owed The Colonel a lot, basically his entire career and the wellbeing of his sister-in-law, Amelia.

"It's about my daughter," The Colonel hedged, clearly uncomfortable.

Ridge's heart stuttered and stopped. "Jane?" If Jane and Blue were having problems, Ridge might lose the best hacker in the industry. It was a selfish thought, but he couldn't seem to help it. Plus Blue was a friend, both to him and to Maggie.

"Not that one. Jane's doing well. You know, I never would have guessed Blue would turn out to be son-in-law material when I plucked him out of that prison, but the boy's grown on me. He makes Jane happy, and he treats her well. No, Jane's not the problem. It's Bailey."

"Bailey, sir?" Ridge asked. The Colonel was notoriously private and protective of his family life, and with good reason. He was a high value target, and that meant his family could always be in danger, too. In fact, until recently, Ridge hadn't known anything about The Colonel's children until they had a case that required Jane's expertise, which The Colonel volunteered. Jane was the middle of three daughters, but Ridge didn't know the names of the others.

"My oldest. She's recently been honorably discharged, and you know what a rough transition that can be."

"Yes, sir." Even shifting from SEAL life to being an undercover agent had been challenging. The military had a way of conditioning people for life.

"She's been living with her mother and me, and, uh, I don't know how to say this, but, uh, well, she's driving me crazy. It's not that I don't love her, I do, but we're too much alike to be under the same roof for this long. Besides that, she needs something, some job or project to take her focus off things until she figures out what she wants to do next."

"Yes, sir," Ridge said, understanding the problem. "How can I help?"

"You're more plugged in to the everyday nitty gritty of what we do. Bailey's a worker. She needs to get her hands dirty to feel good. I want you to keep an ear out. If you hear of anything for her, send it my way."

"Begging your pardon, sir, but this seems contradictory to what you told me about Jane," Ridge said. The Colonel had practically threatened to end him if anything happened to Jane while on his watch.

"The situation is different, and so are the girls. Jane is soft and gentle, a civilian to the core. Bailey can handle herself, and she thrives on the danger, on the adventure. Try to coddle her, and she'll cut you."

"She does sound like you, sir," Ridge said, his eyes alight with amusement.

"The difference is I learned my lessons. The girl's got more courage than brains some days. Ah, this looks delicious," The Colonel said, standing as Maggie rejoined them.

She had purposely lingered in the kitchen, giving the men a chance to talk, Ridge knew. It was a tricky thing to have a higher security clearance than his wife, but Maggie was good about slipping away, about not pressing him to tell her things or trying to finagle information or secrets out of him. Thankfully there weren't many things he couldn't tell her, and this one wouldn't make the list. He would appeal for her help with Bailey Dunbar because Maggie had good people sense. If what The Colonel said about his daughter was true, he would need all of Maggie's intuition and then some.

CHAPTER 2

Two days after the surprise visit from The Colonel, Ridge had another shock—his brother called.

It wasn't that Calhoun never called, but rather that he always called with purpose—Christmas, Thanksgiving, and occasionally a birthday. Cal was six years older and immeasurably tougher. It was telling that Cam was a decorated Navy SEAL, had killed more people than he liked to count, and was still labeled "the sensitive one" in the family.

"What's up, bud?" Cal began, another oddity. He never called simply to chat or exchange pleasantries. Usually they discussed their parents or the ranch or financial matters. As part of his inheritance, Cam owned thirty percent of the ranch. Upon their father's death, he would have to decide if he wanted to continue to maintain his portion or allow Cal to buy him out. For now all his profit from that ownership went into a trust.

"Not much, Cal. How about you?"

"Same here. How's LS?"

LS was Cal's nickname for Maggie, Little Sister. The two hadn't spent much time together, but what they had had been enough to form a mutual adoration society. As she did with everyone, Maggie had a way of bypassing outer defenses and going straight for the heart, even with his straight-laced older brother.

"She's good. The change in seasons had inspired her to bake up a storm."

Instead of the usual jokes about Cam getting fat, Cal surprised him again. "Tell her to send some of it this way. I've been craving pie and babygirl can cook."

"How's Isabel?" Cam asked and inwardly winced at the unintended comparison. Isabel could not cook, nor did she try. He knew Cal loved her, but when side by side with Maggie, his sister-in-law came up cold, shallow, empty, and standoffish.

"Same old, same old."

"How are Mom and Dad?"

"Good. They're heading your way soon, I think."

"They are?" Cam asked. His parents hadn't visited him in forever.

"Maggie," Cal explained.

"Ah," Cam said. Maggie was a magnet, pulling people together, even his parents who hated to fly, apparently. "Are you okay?" Cam chanced.

"Me? Shoot, yeah. Busy, though. I could use some of your SEAL mojo down here. The drug smugglers are wearing a path through the south forty, and I've got rustlers pressing in from the north."

Cam made sympathetic sounds of understanding. In recent years, south Texas had become like a war zone. Not that he worried about Cal. His brother could take care of himself. Someone would have to be crazy to... He stood upright and clutched the phone as a new thought occurred. "Wait, did you say you need help?"

"Never thought you'd hear me admit it, huh? But, yeah, things are a bit dodgy down here. 'Course I know you can't actually come down here and help, but..."

"I might have someone who can. A soldier, recently discharged, looking for some action."

"Shoot, we've got action and then some," Cal said. "What's the guy's name?"

"Bailey," Cam said, purposely omitting her gender. His brother was a good man, rock solid, but also an old-school misogynist. Things could go horribly wrong, but Cam was learning to let go of control, to delegate. The Colonel had said Bailey was like him. If that was the case, she'd likely find a way to prove herself to Cal. And if not, well, DC was a long, safe way from Texas.

CHAPTER 3

Bailey wasn't fooled. She was being dispatched. No one knew her father as well as she did, probably because they were so much alike. He had called one of his contacts and asked him to find something for her to do because she was driving him crazy. Not that she blamed him—she was driving herself crazy. She was not built for inactivity, not cut out for civilian life, and leaving the marines had never been in her plan. She'd intended to go all the way, to rise through the ranks and shatter records. Instead she had been ignominiously, albeit honorably, discharged due to high blood pressure. She had begged, literally begged, her superiors to keep her. They had wanted to, but her body hadn't cooperated. No matter what combination of medicine they gave her, her blood pressure soared higher and higher until she was in near constant danger of stroking out or dropping dead. And so at the age of thirty she was tasked with starting over, of finding a new way of life when the military was all she had ever known, all she had ever loved. *What now?* her mind kept saying, but so far she hadn't been able to find any answers.

So now she found herself heading to south Texas to help a rancher, some distant connection of her father's. It was a pity job, one that forced her into an unknown place among strangers. But it was better than nothing. At least it was a way to fill the long hours and days until she got herself together and figured out what was next. And so far it was leaps and bounds ahead of being confined in the city. Bailey hated DC, or any large city, for that matter. She had grown up mainly in Africa and was used to wide open spaces, to plains and prairies. Except for the oppressive humidity, Texas looked much the same— flat, open, uninhabited. It would be boring with so little to do and nowhere to go, and so far Bailey loved it. She could already feel her blood pressure easing out of the stratosphere it routinely inhabited. Maybe getting away for a while—from home, from people, from buildings and noise and smog—would be enough to fix her, to remedy whatever was going wrong in her body. And if that happened, she could go back to the marines. That was her dream and her goal, to get healthy enough to go back.

She took a commercial flight to San Antonio where a ranch hand met her at the airport. His eyes had scanned the crowd over her head until she was the only one left. "Are you from Ridge Ranch?" she finally asked because he looked like a cowboy—kind of leathery and scrappy with thick boots and a big hat.

He blinked at her in confusion. "Yes, ma'am."

"I'm Bailey," she said, extending her hand.

His grip was tentative when he took it and shook. "You're Bailey, ma'am?"

"Yes, sir," she said, and her grip was not tentative. It took him by surprise so that when he withdrew his fingers, he shook them out, wincing.

"Well," he said. "Well. Doggone." He remained staring at her in consternation a few beats.

"Is there a problem?" she asked, feigning ignorance. Of course there was a problem, and it was always the same problem. She was a woman when she was supposed to be a man, at least in the expectations of others. But Bailey had lived in the realm of men her entire life, and she was used to it, so she let his shock, confusion, and disappointment roll off her back.

"No, ma'am, I just…no ma'am. Let me grab your stuff."

"I've got it, but thank you," she said, tossing her duffle over her shoulder.

"That's it, ma'am?" he asked, showing further surprise at her lone duffle.

"Yes, sir," she said, maintaining eye contact until he looked away. She could tell him she traveled light because it was what years in the military had trained her to do. She could tell him she was low maintenance, only owning a few shirts, pants, and one change of shoes. But explaining and apologizing was a girly thing to do, and Bailey was no one's idea of girly.

"Well, then, come along," the cowboy said. He turned and began threading his way through the airport, Bailey keeping stride beside him. They reached the outside and Bailey sucked a breath, trying to adjust her body from the falsely conditioned air of the airport to the stifling humidity of outside. For her part, she preferred the humidity. Not having grown up with air conditioning, she had never grown accustomed to it. The cowboy reached for her door, intending to open it for her. Then he faced her, uncertain. She gave him a gentle smile. He opened the door for her and held out a hand to help her into the tall truck. She didn't need the hand, but she took it nonetheless.

"Thank you, sir," she said, tossing her duffle onto the seat behind.

"Yes, ma'am," he said, closing the door once she was safely inside.

Manners were nice, and Bailey was always glad for the reminder that chivalry wasn't dead. She wasn't the type of woman who needed help, but neither was she the type of woman to refuse it on principle. *It's nice to be nice,* her mother often said, and Bailey agreed.

"Mind if I listen to the radio?" the cowboy asked.

"No, sir," Bailey said. He tuned the radio to a country station, picked up a soda can from the console, and spit into it. Bailey turned to face the window, hiding her grimace. She could stomach a lot but had never warmed up to tobacco juice. Her stomach churned. She closed her eyes and breathed through her nose until she got herself back under control. She was headed to a rough, unsettled place full of rough, unsettled men, nothing she hadn't handled before. She would stick to herself and keep her own counsel, as she always did.

The ride to the ranch was long and might have been boring, if not for Bailey's aforementioned love of nothing. The scenery outside was blessedly flat and uneventful with both houses and towns few and far between. Mostly there were cattle, lots and lots of cattle.

"How far is the ranch?" Bailey asked, a half hour in.

"This is the ranch, ma'am," he said and Bailey's gaze returned to the window.

"This is all the same ranch?" she asked, another twenty minutes later.

"Yes, ma'am."

She wanted to ask how large it was but figured it was some kind of etiquette breach to do so. And so she kept staring out the window, watching cows and land go by, mile after mile after mile.

Forty minutes later, they arrived at a sprawling ranch house. It looked like something from the old west, Spanish style stucco with two massive annexes sprouting from the center like wings.

"Here we are, ma'am," the cowboy said, unnecessarily so since it was the only house for miles and miles. Bailey reached for her duffle, but the cowboy put up a hand. "Uh, I'd leave that, ma'am, until you talk to Cal. It's, uh, possible you might not be staying."

Bailey suppressed a sigh and heaved herself from the tall truck, landing lightly on her feet. As they approached the house, a man stepped through the front door, filling it completely. He was massive, well over six feet with shoulders so wide they appeared to brush the doorway. But it was his bearing more than his size that told Bailey who he was. She had been in the military long enough to automatically know who was in charge. This man was master of his domain and, guessing from his bearing, possibly the entire world. His gaze swept her up and down—from her tidy ponytail to her polished combat boots—then quickly dismissed her and turned questioningly to her chauffer.

"This is Bailey," the cowboy explained, pointing at her, a hint of nervousness in his tone.

The man's gaze rested once again on Bailey. He tilted his head at her and shook it. "No. Take her back."

"Um, excuse me," Bailey said, taking a step forward. "You were expecting a man. Believe me, I get that a lot, but I'm also a marine, and I heard you're in need of some help."

He smiled at her in an amused sort of way. "Darlin', you're cute. And I'm certain you're good at whatever it is you do, but this is no place for a woman, believe me. So I think it's best for all of us if you go on back home now." He turned dismissively away, not waiting for her reaction.

"No," Bailey said.

The man stopped short and faced her again. "No?"

She shook her head. "I was hired for a job, and I'll decide when it's over. Now, if you'll kindly show me where I'll be staying, I'd like to freshen up."

He took a step forward, his smile disappearing. "You realize I'm the one who's paying you to do the job."

"Yes, sir."

"And if I don't pay you, then there's no job," he said.

"You're going to need me to prove myself. I get that a lot, too. So let me get started, and I'll show you I'm capable. If, after that, you still feel I'm not what you need or want, I'll go away again." Bailey had worked incredibly hard to cut all emotion from her tone over the years because the first one to show emotion lost. And she never lost. So she wasn't angry or hurt, and the injustice of the situation didn't affect her. She kept it reasonable and rational, because that was the only way to win. And Bailey always won.

The big man blinked at her, assessing. "Tell you what, little bit. You take me down right now, and the job is yours."

She blinked at him, the only outward sign of her shock. "You want me to take you down?"

"Yes, ma'am. To the ground, right here, right now, and you can stay."

She licked her lips, her eyes darting to the horizon. "You're not attacking me. It's not ethical to disable a man who's standing still."

"Neither is it easy. So show me what you've got, little one, or go away."

Bailey took a few steps closer so they were approximately six feet apart. Behind her, the cowboy shifted in anticipation and possibly amusement. The man in front of her was certainly amused. "Let me clarify, sir, you want me to take you down to the ground, you're requesting me to do that?"

"I'm demanding it," he said, grinning, not even attempting to hide his laughter at her expense.

"Yes, sir," she said and, before he could blink, withdrew a Taser from her pocket and zapped him. He dropped to the ground, convulsing as the voltage ran through his body. Bailey yanked the bolts out of his chest and retrieved them, standing over him as she did so.

"You zapped me," he said when he could rightly talk again. His voice was tinged with no small amount of pain.

She loomed over him, hands on hips. "First of all, you never said how I had to take you down, only that I had to. Second, I'm five feet and five inches tall, what did you expect? Fight smarter, not harder, that's my motto."

Behind them, the cowboy leaned on his truck and guffawed, gasping in a wheezy manner that told her he probably smoked, too. The man on the ground groaned, whether in pain or defeat Baily didn't know.

"Now, sir, where can I put my things?" Bailey demanded.

CHAPTER 4

Calhoun tried to call his little brother three times with no answer. On the last try, he left a voicemail.

"Boy, next time I see you, you better run," was all he said, but he hoped it was enough to convey all his frustration. A woman. His brother had sent him a woman. Really, what had he been thinking? Had he been away from Texas so long he had forgotten how that would go over? Worse, the woman had bested him, had done the one thing he told her to do to be able to stay. She had cheated, but still, she had done it. And now he was stuck with her, stuck having to explain to thirty cowboys this tiny woman was now in charge of security. They had looked at him like he'd lost his mind. Maybe he had.

At least she was quiet and intelligent. And he liked that she was a marine. He had full respect for the military, and what he said to her was true—he was certain she'd been good in that capacity. But this was Texas, and it was a whole other world. The men under his command would respect her, however grudgingly, but would they listen to her, take her seriously? Doubtful. And then there were those on the other side, brutal, lawless drug smugglers who viewed women as pawns, as playthings, who used them in the worst possible way. Cal was worried she would be one more liability, and his plate was already filled to the max. And then there was the matter of where she would sleep. No way could he put her in the bunkhouse. It was and had always been men only. He had no choice but to put her up in his house. He had plenty of space, enough for her to have her own wing, really, but still. The invasion of privacy left him antsy. And then there was Isabel. What would his wife say when she found out? And she would undoubtedly find out. It was a mess, a big, huge mess, and he had his little brother to blame for it.

"Good morning, everyone," Bailey said to the assembled group of ranch hands before her. A couple of them snickered. Cal gave them a look, and they shut up. "My name is Major Bailey Dunbar, US Marines. If you'd like to know more about my resume, including my time at the Naval Academy, tours of duty and active service, I'd be happy to tell you later. In the meantime, I'd like to spend some time learning from you about the ranch and its specific security needs. In the next few days, I'll be accompanying several of you as you go about your duties, observing, listening, talking. I feel you have a lot to teach me."

One of the hands in the back snickered. Bailey raised an eyebrow at him and pinned him with a stare until his smile faded and he sat up straighter. "I'll begin making rounds first thing tomorrow. In the meantime, I'd like to see your weapons and hear a bit about your experience and expertise with them." When no one moved, she removed her gun from its holster and held it up for their inspection. "This is my weapon of choice, both for sentimental value and utility. It's a Springfield Armory 1911, a gift from my father upon graduation from the Naval Academy. I understand you use shotguns and rifles more often here, and I'll adjust accordingly. But this one will stay with me."

"Can I see it?" Cal surprised everyone including himself by asking. But he was a gun enthusiast, and it was a fine piece.

"Of course," she said, handing it over. He inspected it and handed it back to her.

"Nice piece."

"Thank you. And what do you carry, Mr. Ridge?"

"It's Cal." He reached into his holster and withdrew his weapon, an SVI Tiki-T. Her eyes rounded as she took it, duly impressed.

"It's beautiful," she breathed, and he laughed a little because he'd never seen a woman so awed by a weapon before. She knew her guns, that much was apparent.

After that, everyone felt more at ease with showing her their weapons. She took due time with each, making a careful and calculated inspection, holding it up, testing the weight, viewing the sights, asking questions. The bunkhouse took on a kind of social, party atmosphere with everyone talking weapons and ammo. It was a comfort zone for the men, and for Bailey too, apparently. The common thread was one thing they could relate over, if nothing else. Cal watched her closely, observing, judging. He liked that she wasn't cocky. If anything, she seemed humble, ready and willing to listen. It wouldn't have gone over well for anyone who came in making demands and changes, but especially not for a woman. But coming in gently, humbly, quietly made an impression on the men and they began to open up to her, at least a little.

"Thank you all so much," she said, smiling at them. It helped that she was pretty, Cal conceded, but it was also confusing. How could a woman be both soft and pretty and hard and capable? She was definitely soft and pretty, but maybe she wasn't as hard and capable as she first seemed. Time would tell. He would give her some leeway, a little bit of rope, and hope she didn't hang herself with it.

His foreman, Jinx, took her on a tour of the main portion of the ranch. Jinx reported later she carried a little notebook, wrote things down, asked a few pertinent questions, but otherwise didn't say much.

"She's a cool customer, that one," Jinx said, bestowing his unasked opinion.

"You don't like her?" Cal asked. Jinx had been at the ranch as long as he had, working first for his father before working for him.

"Never said that. Can't quite get a read on her, but she's interestin', real interestin'."

Cal agreed she was a bit of a riddle, but that annoyed him. He was too busy for riddles. He wanted simple and straightforward, someone to come in and do the job that needed to be done without making him puzzle his head and wonder over her.

"Isabel ain't gonna be happy," Jinx added, and Cal's insides tightened.

"Isabel doesn't have a say anymore, does she?" Cal asked.

Jinx shrugged. "She could make the girl's life a misery."

"The girl's seen combat in Afghanistan. I think she can handle Isabel."

Jinx shrugged again, conveying his uncertainty and, despite his words, Cal wasn't certain either. He'd known his wife long enough to be wary of her and her reactions. Bailey might know how to handle men, but could she handle women? Time would tell on that front, too.

At seven he wearily made his way inside for supper. Estralita, his housekeeper, had left him supper on the stove like usual. Unlike usual, someone else now sat at his table. He almost jumped in surprise when he walked in the kitchen and saw Bailey sitting at the table, a notebook and pen open in front of her.

"I'm sorry, would you like me to leave?" she asked, noting his reaction even though he tried to hide it.

"No, it's fine," he lied. In truth, he valued his privacy and wanted nothing more than to be alone. "Have you eaten?"

"No, sir."

"Do you like things spicy?" he asked.

"Yes, sir."

"Then you're in the right place. Dish yourself a bowl of stew and grab some cornbread."

She followed suit, dishing a heaping bowl of stew and laying a hearty slice of cornbread on top. It was a good thing Estralita always made scads too much because apparently Bailey was an eater.

"You're going to have to help yourself while you're here. I don't keep regular hours, and I won't be able to keep track of meals for you," he warned.

"Yes, sir," she agreed. "Do you mind if I grab the butter?"

"Really, help yourself," he said, indicating the fridge with a wave of his hand. He had no idea if they had butter, but he assumed so. Estralita did all the shopping, and she usually kept up on those kinds of things. Bailey opened the refrigerator, pulled out butter and jam and then, to his surprise, went the extra step of dishing them into another container before she set them on the table. It was a feminine thing to do, wholly unexpected by her, and he found himself staring at her, wondering again over her contradictory nature.

She poured herself a sip of tea, tasted it, and grimaced. "Too sweet?" he guessed.

"Yes, sir," she agreed, filling her glass with water instead.

"It grows on you," he said, slightly annoyed for reasons he couldn't discern. Most likely it was because of Isabel. She would never drink the tea, either, always conscious of too many calories.

"Too much sugar makes my brain feel sluggish," Bailey explained. "I prefer to be alert."

"It's not because you're watching your figure?" Cal pressed, earning a slight frown from her.

"No, sir. I've always been too active to worry much about my figure."

"You really don't have to call me sir," he added. "I've never been a soldier, unlike my brother."

"Your brother, sir?" she asked, sitting across from him at the table.

"The guy who got you the job," he said.

"Oh," she drawled. "Sorry, sir, I don't know him. But he probably works for my father."

"Who's your father?" he asked.

"Colonel John Caruthers."

"The Colonel is your dad?" Cal blurted. He had heard of Cam's legendary boss over the years, many times. The man was mythical by now.

"Yes, sir," she said, smiling slightly as if she knew what he thought.

He took a few bites, trying hard not to stare at her. She was such a mystery. "Are you married?"

"No, sir. Are you asking because my name is different than my father's?" He nodded. "Safety precaution, sir. My sisters and I all go by our mother's maiden name."

"Smart," he said. "Why did you leave the marines?"

She sighed. "High blood pressure, sir."

"Are you all right?"

"Yes, sir. It doesn't slow me down."

"I can see that it doesn't," he commented, earning another small smile from her. She was cute with shoulder length brown hair she kept in a tidy ponytail, hazel eyes, and a pretty smile. Occasionally if the smile grew large enough, he caught a flash of dimples. He had the feeling she tried hard to keep those dimples under wraps because she wasn't a dimple kind of girl. She was pretty but not too pretty, certainly no one's idea of beautiful. Not like Isabel, his drop dead, knockout, gorgeous wife.

"May I ask why you're staring at me, sir?" she said, returning his frank and assessing gaze.

"I'm trying to figure you out," he said.

"If you succeed, please let me know. I'm sure my sisters and mother would be happy to hear a firsthand account," she said, and he laughed.

"Not your dad?"

"My dad and I understand each other perfectly, sir," she said.

"Then by all means tell me about your father," he said, knowing instinctively she would loathe talking about herself.

"My father is a soldier first, and everything else comes after. Some people were born to be in the military, and my father is one of those people." She tapped her temple. "It makes perfect sense, sir. The chain of command, the duty, the honor, the service, the sacrifice. It was what he was born for, why he was put on this earth. Without that," she broke off and looked toward the pot of stew, "who is he, really?"

How would Cal feel if he didn't have the ranch? He had played pro football for five years, and he loved football, but it never took the place of the ranch in his heart. He always knew he would come back home and take over for his father. It was in his blood, a way it never had been for his little brother. He knew what it was to have a destiny, to have a lifelong purpose. How would he feel if it got taken away?

When he remained silent, she tore her gaze away from the stew and looked at him. "Thank you."

He blinked at her in surprise. "For what?"

"For not telling me it's going to be okay," she said.

They shared a sympathetic smile of understanding. "Sometimes things aren't okay. Instead they become a new kind of normal, a way to cope, a status quo." His thoughts turned to Isabel then, and he could feel himself sinking.

"Weren't you a quarterback, sir?" she asked, interrupting his thoughts.

Someone had done her homework. "Yes."

"I guess I expected a bit more inspiration, sort of a gridiron type lecture," she said, and he laughed.

"Get it done, Bailey. Be the ball or I'll end you."

"You're incredibly bad at this," she said.

"It's been a while, I'm out of practice," he conceded.

When the meal was finished, Cal put away the food while Bailey did the dishes and wiped the counters. He felt a bit awkward, not certain if he was supposed to try and entertain her, but when he looked up, she had disappeared. He escaped into his office, did about an hour's worth of work and then poured a glass of tea and went to sit on the porch. The sun had already set. It was dark and still. He blamed the darkness for the fact that it took him fifteen minutes to realize Bailey sat in the rocking chair to his right. He flinched, almost spilling his tea.

"Sorry," she murmured. "I wasn't sure if you knew I was here or not."

"I knew," he lied.

"You're a bad liar, sir," she said mildly, and he smiled.

"How old are you Bailey?" he asked. She seemed incredibly young to him, but if she was a major, she had to have been in the marines a while.

"Thirty, sir."

"I remember thirty," he said. He and Is had been married three years then. It was the first time he brought up having children with her, the first time he heard her say she would never have them, ever. It was a fact she'd kept hidden all through the dating process. If he had known, would he still have married her? It was a question that kept him up at night, one of many.

"You can remember back that far, sir?" Bailey asked, and he laughed again.

"I don't think you know me well enough to joke about my age, child. Besides, I'm still in my thirties."

"Hanging on by your fingertips, sir," she remarked, and he snickered.

"A young girl like you is bound to be bored out here," he remarked.

"No, sir."

"Yes, ma'am."

"No, sir."

"Yes, m...we could go on like this a while. Why don't you tell me why a young lady such as yourself will not grow bored here in the middle of nowhere with nothing to do."

"I grew up in Africa, sir. This feels like home, minus the lions."

"We have mountain lions," he said.

"Well, there you go," she said.

They sat in silence a while longer, staring out at the dark, still night. Occasionally her rocking chair squeaked on the floorboard. An owl hooted. Fireflies danced. It was the sort of night Cal loved, and he sensed Bailey did, too. It was hot and humid, oppressively so, but Cal sipped his tea and didn't mind.

"I might change my mind about tea," Bailey said after a while.

"The sugar seems to help with the heat, don't know why," he said and then surprised them both by handing her his glass.

She took a gulp and handed it back. "Thank you, sir."

"Bailey."

"Yes, sir."

"Stop calling me sir. You're making me feel old."

"Old is a state of mind, sir," she replied.

"You're going to do what you want, regardless of what I say, huh?" he asked.

"Yes, sir," she said. "I always do."

"Well, all right then," he said and drained his tea with one final gulp.

CHAPTER 5

The next morning, Bailey beat him out the door. And because he left at five, that was no easy feat. When he saw her at the barn, he realized he hadn't asked her if she could ride and could have kicked himself for the omission. How had he overlooked that most important detail? Because she had him stymied, that's how. She wasn't like anyone he'd ever encountered, and he'd encountered a lot of people. Last night they had experienced an unexpected level of comfort with each other, but even so he never felt like she was flirting with him. He couldn't wrap his mind around her dichotomous nature, and it niggled in his brain, almost but not quite frustrating him. He'd dated a lot of women before Isabel, had been friends with all the girls in town, was still friends with the wives and sisters of his ranch hands. And none of them was anything like this one marine.

He stood far back, watching her with her horse. She bridled it on her own and easily swung up into the saddle, subduing her mount when she grew jittery. If she could do all that, it was likely she could ride, and his mind was at ease. She was on Jinx's watch today anyway; he had far too much to do to play babysitter.

Bailey swung up onto the horse and felt even more like she was coming home. She and her sisters hadn't owned horses when they were children, but a neighbor had. Bailey and the neighbor's daughter had been the same age, and they had ridden together almost daily. She had desperately longed for a horse of her own, but had always moved too much, both as a child and as an adult. Maybe once she got settled, wherever that may be, she would buy a horse of her own. And a dog. She had a cat, and she liked it, but it wasn't the same as a dog or a horse.

"Ready, Miss Bailey?" Jinx asked, interrupting her thoughts.

"Yes, sir," she replied. "Lead on."

"Sure you got enough guns?" he joked. She was armed with the gun she kept in her shoulder holster as well as one on her ankle and a rifle strapped to her back.

She grinned at him. "Always be prepared, that's my motto."

"You ain't like any boy scout I ever saw," he said, kicking his horse into gear.

"Bet you would have joined up, if I were," she said.

Now it was his turn to smile. "Yes'm."

They took off, heading onto the vast openness of the ranch. Bailey wasn't naturally good with directions, but she had taught herself to be so by paying attention and focusing. Today they headed west, away from the sunrise, much to Bailey's disappointment. This was her first glimpse of Texas, and she'd heard the sunrises were legendary. They rode due west for about an hour before heading north. They still hadn't reached the edge of the ranch's property, according to Jinx, but he wanted to show her where the rustlers were stealing cows in the northwest quadrant.

"This here's the place, ma'am," he said.

She got down off her horse and walked around for a bit, relishing the feel of land for a change. She was in good shape, but riding for ninety minutes solid used a whole other set of muscles than she was used to.

"Walk me through the process, Jinx. The cattle get stolen, the brand gets changed, and then what happens?"

"They get sold off on a black market internet auction and shipped to another country," he said.

"If they get sold off and shipped, what's the purpose of changing the brand?" Bailey asked.

"In case anybody bothers to stop and do a brand inspection. It's supposed to happen when the cows leave the lot, but sometimes money slips hands, you know what I mean?"

"Hmm. Does Mr. Ridge own an airplane?" she asked.

"Yes, but the guy who flies it isn't always available."

"He doesn't fly it himself?"

Jinx grinned at her. "Scared to fly. Don't tell him I told you. Like to near killed him when he had to fly east for Cam's wedding."

She smiled, too. It was hard to imagine Calhoun Ridge afraid of anything. Not only was he tall, broad, and well-muscled, but he had that sort of vibrant energy that took over any space he occupied. "Our secret."

"Miss Bailey," Jinx said when she continued to scan the horizon.

"Yes, sir?" she asked, shading her eyes as she squinted up at him.

"Are you purposely prolonging things so you won't have to get back in your saddle?"

"Am I that transparent, Jinx?" she asked.

"Only to an old hand who's done the same thing," he said.

"It's been a long time since I rode. My muscles aren't accustomed to it."

"You're going to be plenty sore tomorrow," he said. "I suggest we take the truck next time."

"Jinx, might we have taken the truck today and you were testing me to see if I could ride?"

"Yes, ma'am," he said with no hint of apology.

"How'd I do?" she asked.

"You're a little soft, but you're no greenhorn."

"High praise from the likes of you," she said.

"Yes'm," he agreed.

Steeling herself for the inevitable pain, she took a deep breath and swung into the saddle again.

They returned to the ranch in time for lunch. Bailey was exhausted, but the day was far from over. She scrounged lunch in

Cal's kitchen and made herself a few notes on the morning's activities. After that she and Jinx took the truck to the trouble spot to the south, the one where the cartels were smuggling drugs.

"There's an actual road," she noted, her eyes following the gravel path that ran from southwest to northeast, the perfect route for smugglers, both of drugs or people.

"Yes'm, and it's caused us no end of trouble."

"What about border patrol, ICE?"

Jinx laughed humorlessly. "Now you sound like a greenhorn. Miss, we are and have been locked in a land war for the last century, since this ranch first began. No one besides the people who live here actually cares what goes on. To them it's all just political wrangling. But to us it's our livelihoods and safety. When I was a kid, people came through this road, good people, hard working people looking for a job. We paid them to do a hard day's labor, and they took it back home to their families. Now only two types of people come through here—desperate and dangerous. The desperate ones are willing to do whatever it takes to get by. The dangerous ones, well, there's really no limit to what they might do. Our place has been safe, probably 'cause they're a mite scared of Cal and his big size and mean temperament. But that can only last so long afore things go south. It's an uneasy peace we have going, but it feels like any minute it could break."

It was a long speech for the solitary man, but Bailey appreciated the input. "What would happen if Cal made the first strike?"

"They'd strike back, bigger and harder."

"Will he retaliate if something is done to him?"

"Depends on what's done. If it's property or money, he'll let it go. If it's people, that's a whole other matter."

Maybe it came from Jinx and his words, but it felt as though the whole place radiated with tension and anxiety, a pile of kindling in search of a spark. "What do you suppose would happen if the first strike was something soft and subtle, not an out and out act of war but more of a micro-aggression?" she asked.

"I can't rightly say, Miss Bailey. These people, and I hesitate to call them that because they act more like animals, these cartels, hacking people to pieces and putting their heads on pikes, they don't operate like you and me. They have their own rules."

Bailey was all too acquainted with the brutality of men. She'd seen it in action in combat, had seen some of the worst things men could do to each other with little to no provocation. She would have to tread carefully, much more than she first realized.

"Thank you, Jinx. This has been most informative," she said.

"You talk real purdy, miss," he said, tossing her a wink.

"Are you flirting with me?" she asked.

"Never could I ever resist a pretty girl," he answered. Then, wonderingly, "That's probably why I ended up with seven children."

Bailey laughed out loud, and he smiled at her amusement. "Do any of them work the ranch?"

"All four boys," he said. "The girls never took to it. I tried dadgum hard to get one or two of them married off to Cam or Cal but," he shook his head sadly, "they all had other ideas. Can't make kids do what you want them to for nothin'."

"I'm sure my parents would sympathize with you," she said.

"Well, now, I'm sure your parents must be real proud of you, Miss Bailey, a marine major and all."

"Yes, but I'm not anymore," she said, her smile dimming as she turned to look out the window.

"Well, you were, and that's somethin'," he said, his tone brooking no argument.

"Thank you, Jinx," she said. "Where might I find the key to the airplane?"

"Cal keeps it in his office."

"Think he'll let me take it up for a spin?" she asked.

"Long as you don't ask him to go with you, I don't see why not," Jinx said. They shared a smile, and he turned up the radio, singing along to a happy country tune.

CHAPTER 6

Cal was in his office when Bailey tapped softly on his door.

"May I take your airplane?" she asked.

He tore his eyes away from the computer screen, blinking at her while his brain tried to adjust. "Take it where?"

"In the air, for a spin," she said in the tone of someone who thought maybe his brain wasn't working quite right.

"You're a pilot?" he blurted.

Her lips tightened, and he guessed he had offended her. He could almost see the list of possible retorts flashing before her eyes, something like, "Lots of women are pilots now." Instead she simply said, "Yes, sir."

He gave her a knowing, teasing smile. It wasn't that she was a woman so much that she was so doggone cute. Her hair was up in the spunky little ponytail again, only today she'd added a baseball cap up top. She wore a gray t-shirt with tidy denim jeans. In fact all of her was tidy. It was hard to picture her with a hair out of place or a spot of food on her clothes, almost as if those things wouldn't dare, not on her watch.

"Was there anything else you wanted to add, Major Dunbar?" he asked, taunting her to say what was on her mind.

"Would you like to come with me, sir?" she asked, eyes slightly narrowed.

Now his did the same. "Why do you ask?"

She shrugged. "It's your airplane and your ranch. Thought you might like the birds-eye view."

"I'm good, thanks," he said.

"Hmm," she replied with what he could only imagine to be a taunting kind of smile since she wouldn't say so directly. Someone must have talked and told her his Achilles heel—flying. Probably Jinx who for some reason found any hint of humanity in him hilarious.

He tossed her the keys to the plane. "Have at it, little bit."

Her lips tightened again, signaling her dislike for the nickname.

"Anything to add?" he prompted.

She blinked three times and shook her head. "No, sir."

"You are quite a marvel, Bailey. A woman who knows how to keep her mouth closed," he said.

"And you are exactly as expected sir—a man who doesn't know when to shut up." She clutched the keys in her palm, turned on her heel, and disappeared, forcing herself to take measured steps as she walked away from him. She didn't hate the man, but he certainly could irritate her, when he wanted to. She had never done well with being teased, especially not for being small, something she didn't like to be. It was intensely aggravating to feel powerful on the inside but be cute and cuddly on the outside. Calhoun Ridge wasn't all out resisting her, but neither had he fully accepted her presence. Instead he seemed to be indulgently humoring her, and that was almost worse. She could stomach rejection a whole lot better than conde-scension.

But neither would she allow herself to fall prey to the temptation to prove herself. *Steady,* she cautioned. She would not win him over by flying off the handle in an overeager attempt to show him how good she was. All she could do was keep on keeping on and let her work speak for itself. In the meantime, she got to fly.

"This place is amazing," she admitted as she tucked herself in the cockpit and began doing her pre-flight check. It had horses and flat, open prairie, and an airplane. Those were pretty much all of her favorite things in life. Her blood pressure felt better than it had in months. Her head hadn't pounded since she arrived and the tight feeling in her chest and arms had all but disappeared.

She started the plane, and a few of the ranch hands came out to watch. Bailey resisted the urge to wave at them, but it was hard because she was so happy to be flying again. It had been ages. In DC she had little access to a plane and they were overly picky about her health. Technically she wasn't supposed to fly until she got her blood pressure fully under control. But that wasn't a problem here, and her heart soared with the freedom of it all. This was one of the last bastions of true freedom in the entire country, acres upon acres of private land to do whatever she wanted. No flight plan, no flight tower, no fussy federal regulations. Just simple, old-school flying in a tiny beat up plane.

She took off and circled, climbing higher and higher until she was sure she had cleared the tree line. She needed to be low enough to look out but high enough to keep her altitude. When she felt she'd achieved perfection, she made a few concentric circles around the outskirts of the ranch, noting buildings and other landmarks. When she was satisfied with her aerial tour, she headed for the two trouble spots—the north where the rustlers stole cows and the south where smugglers brought drugs.

Finally, when she ran out of reasons to stay up, she circled back around and set it down. Cal was there when she stepped out, and she wasn't certain if it was coincidence or on purpose. "See anything interesting?" he asked.

"I suppose it depends on the definition," she said. "I'd like to get into town, speak with the local law enforcement."

"When?"

"As soon as possible," she said.

"I have some things I need to do tomorrow. You can ride with me."

"Thank you," she said.

"Are you always so polite, Bailey?"

"Yes, sir."

"You're a puzzle, little bit."

"Yes, sir," she agreed.

"Heard that before, have you?" he guessed.

"Yes, sir," she agreed.

"Has anyone ever solved the riddle?" he asked.

"Not to my knowledge, sir," she said.

He opened his mouth to say something, thought better of it, and closed it again. "Hungry?" he tried instead.

"Enough to eat the paste off wallpaper," she said.

"We'll see if we can do a bit better than that." They turned and began heading toward the house in silence. It was a comfortable silence, and both of them were a bit surprised by that. Neither liked to share space, and yet in two days they had fallen into an easy companionship. They ascended the porch steps. Cal reached for the door, but it was pulled open from the inside.

A woman stood in the doorway observing them, her beautiful face cool and composed. Finally she spoke. "Well, I see I've been replaced. That didn't take long."

An ugly sort of tension radiated between the two. Bailey glanced questioningly at Cal. "Bailey, this is my wife, Isabel."

"How do you do?" Bailey asked, extending a hand Isabel ignored completely.

"I do very well," Isabel said, her tone as cold as her expression.

Bailey dropped her hand and crossed her arms over her chest. Obviously something was going on between the husband and wife. Whatever it was, it was none of her concern and couldn't be improved by input from her.

"What do you want, Is?" Cal asked.

"Just dropping by, seeing what the cat dragged in." Her eyes landed on Bailey again.

"Bailey's working for me," Cal said.

"I'm sure she is," Isabel replied.

"Enough," Cal said, the word cold and final. "What do you want?"

"I can't come to my own house? It is still mine, you remember. Well, half."

"If you'll excuse me, I'll go wash up," Bailey said. She took a step toward the door, but Isabel made no move to let her pass. "Or I could stay here and continue to linger awkwardly in your private conversation."

Finally, Isabel stepped to the side and let her through.

"Isn't she the cutest?" Bailey heard her ask, but she skirted around the hallway before she heard Cal's answer.

"Don't," Cal said. "She's an employee, nothing more."

"She's living in our house," Isabel said.

"In her own room, in her own wing, a fact I'm sure you're well aware of since you likely snooped before we got here."

"Oh, honey, you know me so well," Isabel said.

"I certainly do," Cal said, bumping by her to enter the house. With Isabel there, it felt cold and tense again, sharp contrast to the warm, welcoming way it felt without her. How had he ever thought she would fit in this place? In this world?

"I need more money," Isabel said, following him to the kitchen while he washed his hands in the sink.

He laughed humorlessly. "I bet you do. What happened to the twenty thousand I gave you eighteen months ago?"

She shrugged. "Living is expensive."

"The way you do it, maybe," he said.

"Let's review, Cal. Either give me the allowance I want to live on, or I take half the ranch in a divorce. Tossing me a few bucks here and there seems like a much cheaper, easier alternative, don't you think?"

He sighed. "Don't you ever get tired of being so...you?"

"You'd think so, but no. And a lot of people think I'm pretty great, actually."

"That's because they don't have to live with you or pay your bills," he countered.

"Aw, save the banter for your new little toy. She looks like the kind that would enjoy it."

"How much?" he asked.

"Ten thousand," she said.

He bit down on his tongue, swallowing the reaction she wanted from him. She was spoiling for a fight, he could tell. Her cavalier attitude about Bailey covered a mound of jealousy and possessiveness. "I'll think about it," he managed.

"Think hard, Cal, because the more I sit out there alone in my little corner of the world, the more I begin to wonder what I need you for. I could totally run this place."

"You'd run it to the ground in three months," he said, gritting his teeth hard against his growing anger and frustration. Had he ever loved her? It was hard to remember.

"Totally worth it to see you suffer. And then I'd sell the land, bit by bit, take all that money, and go somewhere tropical. Or maybe European. I haven't decided yet."

"Go away, Isabel," he said. "And I don't mean just now. Go far away, leave this place, and forget it ever existed."

She smiled and tapped his wedding band. "Not sure you actually mean that. But when you do, it'll be a fun conversation with my lawyer. All that football money, just languishing in an account somewhere. My, my, won't that be fun."

He swallowed hard, his Adam's apple bobbing, the vein in his temple throbbing. Isabel was the only woman he had ever been tempted to hit. He had never done it, would never do it, but the temptation always left him feeling shaken. What kind of man even thought about hitting a woman? No kind he had ever wanted to be, and yet here he was.

"Do it," Isabel whispered, reading his thoughts. "And then I'll have you arrested and take you for even more."

"I would never hit you, and you know it. But even if I did, you'd be hard pressed to find someone to arrest me around here. You're nobody's favorite."

"I wouldn't say that," she said with a taunting little smile.

"Is there anything I can do to help with supper?" Bailey asked, and it was as if somebody pulled the plug on his frustration. He took a deep breath, one that reached all the way to the bottom of his lungs this time, and turned his back on Isabel.

"I'm sure it's already done. Estralita always leaves us in good shape. Isabel, you can see yourself out, I take it."

"Sure you don't want to count the silver?" she asked.

Cal didn't reply. It wasn't the silver he cared about, and she knew it. If a few trinkets would appease her, he'd gladly hand them over. But Isabel wanted to hit him where it would hurt the most; she wanted the ranch. And she'd get it over his dead body. When she failed to get a reply from him, she turned her attention to Bailey.

"Well, it was such a pleasure to meet you, you little cutie. Take good care of Cal here, but not too much. He's still a married man, after all, and judges don't take a shine to infidelity."

"Seems like you'd know all about that," Bailey replied evenly and Isabel blinked at her, surprised.

"Well, then. Consider the gauntlet tossed, I suppose."

"I'm here for a job. I don't concern myself with trivialities and nonessentials," Bailey said.

"Kudos on picking one who can hold her own. This ought to be fun," Isabel said. "You two have a pleasant meal getting your taste buds burned off by yet another one of Estralita's stews." She wheeled and floated out of the kitchen, actually floated as if her heel-clad feet didn't touch the floor. Bailey had never been capable of floating like that, but neither did she want to. And she had certainly never worn heels. Floating and combat boots were incompatible.

They waited to speak until the front door opened and closed. "Sorry about that," Cal said. He sounded exhausted.

"You doing all right there, boss?" she asked.

He nodded and then changed his mind and shook his head.

"Want to talk about it?" she offered. He sat and she dished stew and bread for each of them, pouring them both a generous glass of sweet tea.

"No, but I suppose there are a few things you need to know to protect yourself."

"It's all right, I'm aces at self-defense," she said, and he smiled.

"I'm afraid you might need more than that with her. It's probably not a surprise to you we're separated, considering she no longer lives here."

"How long?" Bailey asked.

"Two years. As you correctly guessed, she cheated on me and moved out soon after. But even before that things weren't good. I honestly can't remember if they ever were. And I'm part of it, part of the reason she acts like that. It seems like the two of us bring out the worst in each other, and it's been all out war from the beginning."

"I'm sorry to hear that," Bailey said sincerely.

"The thing is, nobody knows about the separation. Not in my family, anyway. A year and a half ago my brother got married and I paid her twenty thousand dollars to fly east for the wedding and pretend we were still together."

"Why?" Bailey exclaimed.

"I don't know. At the time we'd only been separated six months, and I had hope maybe things would work out and we'd get back together. And then I saw Maggie and Cam together, remembered how it's supposed to be, and realized I didn't actually want Isabel back. I mean, I wanted to maintain my marriage because that's what you do— you get married and you stay married. But I can't stand her. She repulses me on every level. The ranch is a pawn between us, the threat she constantly dangles before me. I'm the fourth generation in my family to run this place. Do you understand what it would be like to lose it because I married for looks?"

"Yes," she said, and he thought maybe she did get it. She seemed the type of person who would understand the full weight of the responsibility he was under, of duty and honor.

"What's the solution?" he asked earnestly. "Because so far I can't find my way out, so we linger in this mutual trap of loathing, both of us in misery. She lives on a far corner of the land and dates other men. Lots of other men, if the rumors are true. I remain here, a cuckolded laughing stock who pays for her lavish, entitled lifestyle."

"Have you spoken to a lawyer?"

"Yes, and the law's on her side. She could take half the ranch. I only own seventy percent, my brother owns thirty. In the case of a divorce,

Isabel and I would split my half, thirty five percent each. Even with Cam and I having the majority, she would make life a misery just because she could. She would fight me every step of every day. She would ruin me, ruin the ranch, just because she hates me that much."

"What if you sold all your percentage to your brother before filing for a divorce?" she asked.

"That's called dissipation of assets and, while not technically illegal, it's unethical and frowned upon."

"So is infidelity," she said. "I'm not saying she should walk away with nothing here, but if you sold to your brother, you could give her half the cash value of the ranch. I think any judge would see that as fair. It's not like she'd be empty handed, and I'm guessing you'd rather see the cash go than your family land."

"That's true," he said. "And Cam has enough in his trust to cover at least Is's half of the ranch. I could pay him back in increments."

"Of course it would mean having to tell him the truth."

"I'm guessing by your disapproving tone you believe I should have done that from the beginning," he said.

"I'm a marine. We're kind of big on the truth," she said. "You know, honor, faithfulness, etcetera."

"Sounds like I should have married a marine and saved myself the trouble of a beauty queen," he said.

"Yes, sir," she agreed, and he laughed.

"Tell me, little bit, if you're so hep on marines, why aren't you married to one?"

"Two marines in one family, that's a tricky combination, sir. And I've never found a civilian who measures up."

"Measures up to what?" he asked.

"My exacting standards," she said.

"As someone who chose poorly, let me commend you on that and advise you not to settle," he said.

"Yes, sir," she agreed, and they finished their meal in contemplative silence.

CHAPTER 7

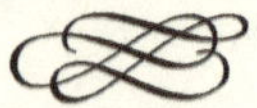

The next morning Cal drove Bailey to town, more than an hour away. Bailey stared quietly out the window the entire time while Cal drank his coffee and tried to wake up. It had been a sleepless night after Isabel's visit; it always was. Regret had a way of keeping him awake, regret and pain and worry for the future. He'd wasted a decade of his life on a woman who didn't love him, who refused to give him children. There was no way to get those years back, no way to make amends for the damage he'd done to himself. The only thing he could do from here was to protect the remainder of his family from Hurricane Isabel.

He returned his coffee to the console and saw Bailey's hand resting idly between them. All of a sudden he was tempted to reach out and take it, and he was both surprised and repulsed by the temptation. He was the sort of man who demanded perfection from himself and usually got it—perfect discipline, perfect control, perfect performance. So it always came as something of a surprise when some wild urge sprang out of him—the desire to hit Isabel, the desire to take Bailey's hand and, not just that, but to reach for her, to pull her to his side of the truck and kiss her. It had been a long time since he kissed

Isabel and even longer since he kissed anyone else. And he missed it, missed the intimacy of being with a woman, both physically and otherwise. He missed sharing his life with someone. Was he attracted to Bailey merely because she was handy or was it something deeper? Either way, she was off limits to him. His wedding band served as a constant reminder of that.

So deep was he in his thoughts about her that he jumped like a nervous jackrabbit when her hand landed lightly on his arm.

"I think you missed our stop, boss."

He came to and looked around, realizing as he did so that he'd driven straight through town. "Sorry, my mind was," he turned to face her, his glance falling to her lips, "somewhere else."

"Hmm," she replied and turned her gaze out the window. He began to wonder how many things she said when she did that because she did it a lot, in multiple different tones. "Who am I meeting with today?"

"Sully Langford, our local Texas Ranger," he said.

"I've never met a Texas Ranger before," she said, perking up.

Cal fought an unwarranted stab of jealousy. She was young and single and could meet with whomever she wished. Meanwhile he was old and married, a broken down has-been quarterback bent on saving his family ranch. Maybe that was it; maybe he was merely jealous of the promising young life ahead of her. She could settle down, have kids, be deliriously happy while his life stretched out before him in a yawning wake of Estralita's stews and quiet nights on the porch.

"Would you like to come with me?" she offered.

He imagined himself as the lone old guy in the room while she and Sully talked. "Thanks, but I have a few things to do. Meet me at the diner in an hour for lunch."

"Yes, sir," she said, sarcastically this time.

"Please," he added belatedly. "Although if you knew me better, you'd know that was implied. When I'm bossing you around, you'll know it."

"I believe it completely, sir," she said.

"Stop calling me sir," he said.

"Yes, sir," she replied.

"Were you this impertinent in the marines?" he asked.

"Subversively so, yes, sir," she replied.

"It's a good thing you've met me at this late and settled stage in my life, Major, because twenty years ago, you and I would have gone a few rounds."

"Then I am incredibly thankful I'm meeting you now instead of then. Would have been a shame to skunk you on your home turf," she said and slipped out of the tall truck, landing lightly on her feet.

Cal remained in the cab a few minutes, draining the last dregs of his now-tepid coffee. His right hand reached for the ring on his left, twisting it. He was tempted to remove it, to take it off and have done with the nightmare that was Isabel and their failed marriage. But removing the ring wouldn't erase the past, wouldn't make Isabel go away, wouldn't change the fact that he was still married to her. With a sigh he dropped his hands. The ring would stay as long as Isabel was still his wife, his albatross, his constant reminder of a mistake that couldn't be undone. Taking a breath, he opened the door and strode from the truck, wondering as he did so how it was going with Bailey and Sully.

*B*ailey was shown into an office to wait for Sullivan Langford. When he finally arrived, she stood. He gave her a patronizing smile that right away set her teeth on edge.

"Have a seat, Miss," he said.

"It's Major," she replied.

"Miss Major?" he asked.

"Major Bailey Dunbar, United States Marine Corp," she held out her hand and he shook it.

"Ah, they're letting women be majors now. Super."

"Yes, sir. We're hoping someday they'll let us vote and drive."

"Oh, you're one of those," he said, sitting down behind his desk.

"One of what, sir?" she asked, remaining standing until he indicated the chair for her with a wave of his hand.

"A feminist."

"No, sir," she contradicted. "I'm merely an American who believes in equality."

"Equal opportunity does not mean equal ability, Miss Dunbar," he said.

"No, sir, I agree with you. Take us for example. You and I have been given equal opportunity, and I'm the only one who's a major," she said.

"Well, ma'am, I'm a Texas Ranger, so I believe I'm doing all right," he said.

"There we can agree, sir," she said, letting go in order to move things along. It would do no one any favors to make an enemy of this man, especially not when she was about to ask a favor of him.

"What can I do for you today?" he asked, his tone more brusque than when he first sat down.

"I'm recently employed by Calhoun Ridge, looking into some security matters on his ranch."

He blinked at her. "Cal hired you? A woman?"

She rested her hands on his desk and leaned forward. "Mr. Langford, let's clear something up. In addition to not having a Y chromosome, I also hold a degree in Operations Research from the Naval Academy where I graduated with honors and distinction after being in the top ten percent of my class. I have served in three active duty combat scenarios overseas, participated in more classified missions than you have teeth, and have eleven confirmed kills to my name. I'm an expert marksman, and I can fly both an airplane and a helicopter. So if you would like to discuss which brand of makeup I prefer or maybe find out how I like to wear my hair or which shopping mall interests me most, I'm happy to do that at a later time. For now, maybe we could stick to the reason I'm here and talk about my job."

"You're a mite touchy about your gender, Miss Dunbar," he said.

"No, Ranger Langford, I'm a mite touchy about everything," she said. She pulled out her notebook and plopped it on the table between them. "I've been surveying the ranch and taking notes, and I have some questions I'd like you to answer."

"I don't think you said the magic word," he replied, and all of a sudden she realized he was flirting with her.

"Oh, geez," she said, pressing her thumb between her eyes to push back the encroaching headache. She could feel her blood pressure rising perilously. "Dismemberment, how's that for a word?"

"Tsk," he made a noise of disapproval, shaking his head. "All that passion and anger needs a proper channel, Major Dunbar."

"Is this real life? I come to you as a professional and you treat the meeting like a speed dating session."

"No one said the two had to be mutually exclusive. Have lunch with me, and we'll talk all you want about your little project on the ranch."

"I'm already committed to lunch with Mr. Ridge, thank the good Lord."

"Cal won't mind, he's a friend of mine."

"My condolences to him," she said, and he laughed.

Bailey gathered her notebook and stood.

"Wait, we never got to have our little talk," he said, still smiling at her in the aggravating way.

"Forget it. I'll handle it myself," she said and without waiting for a response stalked out the front door, slamming it so hard behind her the glass rattled.

Once on the street she rounded the corner and sat on a bench, breathing deeply to get herself back under control. Spots popped behind her closed eyes, and she figured her blood pressure was in or beyond the danger zone by now. The seat beside her squeaked. She braced herself in case it was the obnoxious ranger.

"Everything all right, little bit?" Cal asked.

Bailey opened her eyes and looked up at him. He frowned. "Hey there, what's wrong?" The concern in his tone was genuine, and she could feel her blood beginning to recede back from her brain to where it was supposed to be. She took another deep breath and let it out slowly.

"Sometimes, Mr. Ridge, it's very frustrating to have an outside that doesn't match my inside, to constantly have to prove myself to everyone, to be looked at as little, helpless, and cute. Men seem to believe if I'm not interested in them I must be a lesbian because of course it couldn't be that I simply want to do my job with no distractions. I can't be soft or show any emotion without being dismissed as a little girl. I can't be hard and unyielding without being branded a feminist witch. To always be too much of something for one group of people and never enough of something for everyone else. I know who I am and what I'm about, but I get very weary of a world that tries to make me forget."

He was quiet a few beats before he spoke. "You should have been a quarterback, Bailey, because that was a good speech, one of the best. And I'm sorry I was one of those people who doubted you, who made you have to prove yourself. I promise not to do so again, and I'll give you whatever support you need to do what you came here to do."

"Thank you, sir," she said.

"Stop calling me sir."

"Yes, sir."

He smiled. "Want me to beat up Sully for you?"

"I can do it myself, sir," she said, and he laughed.

"I believe that you could, and I'd kind of like to see it," he said.

"Give it time," she said, and he laughed again.

"Ready for lunch?" he asked.

"Yes, sir."

"The diner is…people are going to talk about us."

"What will they say?" she asked.

"That we're a thing, that I'm using you to get back at Isabel, that I brought you on because you're pretty and I want you in my bed."

"Okay," she said, nodding once decisively.

"Okay?"

"People will talk, sir. It's the nature of things. As long as they don't say I'm incompetent, I don't care what they say."

"I don't think your competence will be foremost in people's minds," he said.

"It's always foremost in mine," she said.

"Very good. Keep focused on that and block out everything else," he prompted.

"I always do, sir," she said, and they walked side by side to the diner.

CHAPTER 8

"I've spent the last few days inspecting the ranch, making observations, talking to people, and taking an aerial view, and I have some thoughts."

"Yes?" he prompted. If there was a hint of defensiveness in his tone, it was because he was so incredibly protective of his ranch.

"First of all, I want you to know I think it's spectacular. I don't think you can appreciate the beauty of flat nothingness unless you've grown up with it. It reminds me so much of home, and I've really enjoyed my time there."

"Thank you, but this sounds a bit like a benediction."

"Not a benediction, simply a frank assessment. Your ranch is beautiful, Mr. Ridge, and I enjoy it immensely."

"Thank you," he said, relaxing a bit. *Oh, geez, she's working me over and doing it well.* "Have you ever considered politics, Bailey? I think you'd have a good shot at being president."

She rolled her eyes. "I'd spend ninety percent of my presidency saying, 'Yes, I am a woman, what of it?'" They shared a smile and she continued. "You believe you have two problem areas on the ranch—the rustlers in the north and the smugglers in the south. I submit to you they're the same problem."

"You think the cartels are stealing my cows?" he asked, eyebrows raised.

"Not exactly, but I think the endgame is the same—drug money. One way or another, and I'm not sure how yet, but I think both things are connected to drugs. One we know for sure is a seller, the smugglers. I find it highly possible that the rustlers are buyers."

"When you put it together like that, I can see it. We've had a raging drug problem here, like everywhere."

"I have some ideas about increasing patrols, including an air patrol by me, and mixing up your schedule and routine. Vary feeding times, etcetera. I think that might be enough to stem the thieves who are looking for a quick, easy buck. Let's not make it quick or easy."

"Sounds good," he said.

"Now, about the smugglers. Clearly it's a tense, complex situation that's going to require a light touch. I don't want to do anything to start a war, but I do think there are some subtle ways we can make things harder for them."

"Like what?"

"How would you feel about unflattening that nice, flat road?" she asked.

"What do you mean?"

"I mean right now it's like a paradise of flat land and easy walking. Let's make it not easy." She huffed a frustrated little sigh. "I really wanted to talk to that Ranger, get his input on the situation, but he's apparently less than useless."

"And speak of the devil, here he is," Cal said as Sully Langford pulled up a chair and joined their table.

"Have you really killed eleven people, or is that something you say to impress people?" he asked Bailey.

"The people who would be impressed by that aren't people I want in my inner circle," she said.

"I'm impressed."

"Then my statement stands," she said.

"Where'd you find this one, Cal?" Sully asked. "Wait, I bet Cam sent her, didn't he? That's funny. Y'all always were for pranks."

"Why would that be a prank?" Cal asked.

"Because she's a woman," Sully said.

"She is?" Cal said, looking at Bailey in dismay. "Son of a gun, you're right."

"Now, I know we got off on the wrong foot, Miss Dunbar," Sully added. Bailey narrowed her eyes at him. "Major Dunbar. But I'm willing and able to have that conversation with you. How's tonight sound?"

"Do you often work at night, Ranger Langford?" she asked.

"Only when I plan to combine business with pleasure," he said.

Bailey wasn't sure what her face looked like, but Cal laughed at her expression. "Careful, Sully, or I just might let her take you outside."

"Now, Cal, you know I could never hit a woman," Sully said.

"Lucky for you I feel the same," Bailey replied. "Excuse me, please." She pushed back from the table and went to the restroom, and it wasn't her imagination that all eyes were on her, whether it was because she was new or because she was at a table with Cal and Sully she didn't know.

"Boy, howdy, she's a case, isn't she?" Sully asked after she was safely gone.

"She's all right," Cal said mildly and Sully's eyes strayed from the door of the bathroom to him.

"You really don't have a type do you, Cal?"

"It's not like that Sully. She's an employee. And, you know..." he held up his ring finger for Sully's inspection.

Sully snorted. "You're the only one hanging on in that relationship. You know who Isabel is dating now?"

"No, and I don't want to," Cal said.

"Well, the new girl is about as far from Isabel as you can get, that's for certain," Sully said.

"She's an employee, Sully. That's all."

Sully grinned. "So you won't mind if I ask her out."

"I thought you already did," Cal said.

"Nah, that's just horseplay. I mean I'd make a real move, kind of show her what I've got."

"It's a free world, Sully. Best of luck to you," Cal said. He would have tipped his hat to him, but he wasn't wearing it.

Bailey returned from the bathroom, saw Sully still at their table, and barely refrained from grimacing.

"What about supper tomorrow?" Sully asked.

"What about it?" Bailey said.

"You and me, I'll show you the town."

"I've seen the town, twice in fact," Bailey replied.

"Come on, we'll talk, compare notes about Cal's ranch, keep it professional."

"Hard pass, Ranger Langford. Hard, hard pass," she said before turning her attention back to Cal. "If it's all the same to you, I think I'll wait outside."

"It's midday. You're going to have to learn a thing or two about Texas heat if you're going to survive," Sully volunteered.

"This is a fine time to practice. Excuse me." She pushed back from the table again and walked out of the diner.

"Butter don't melt in her mouth," Sully said.

"Know your audience, Sully," Cal advised.

"What's that mean?"

"It means you insulted her in every possible way today," Cal said.

"I was just bein' friendly, warnin' her about the Texas sun," Sully huffed.

"She grew up in Africa. I think she knows a thing or two about shade," Cal said, shaking his head. He threw some bills on the table. "Better bring the A game next time."

"That was my A game," Sully muttered.

"That's what makes it so sad," Cal said. He flicked Sully's hat, gave his shoulder a sympathetic pat, and went to find Bailey.

Cal and Bailey drove for a while in silence before anyone spoke.

"I have to say I'm fairly disillusioned in the Texas Rangers," she said at last.

"Sully's all right," Cal said. "You flummoxed him, is all."

"Me? What did I do?"

He glanced at her. She wasn't like anyone Sully had ever encountered. She wasn't like anyone *he* had ever encountered. "He's used to a certain response from women. He's what you'd call our town's most desirable male."

"Him? I thought it would be…" she trailed off and glanced out her window.

"What?"

"Nothing."

"Were you going to say you thought it would be me?" he asked.

She shrugged.

"Why, Major Dunbar, I never. I think I may be blushing. Or maybe you are."

"I don't blush," she said.

"Sure you do, pink cheeks." He poked her leg; she batted his hand away.

"Once a very long time ago that was me. I was a young prince, son of a wealthy rancher, football star, hot-headed, full of myself, certain. And then I went away to college and five years of pro football and sort of lost track of myself. Are you familiar with the story of Esau?"

"From the bible?" she asked. He nodded. "Vaguely, sir."

"He was supposed to be the child of promise, but Jacob stole his blessing. And then he went off and married a woman from outside his religion, outside his culture. So far outside she became a curse on his family. I find the older I get, the more I identify with Esau. Every year, little by little, more and more of that cocksure boy I used to be withers and dies. That dashing young football player is gone. In his place is a broken down, scarred old cowboy."

"I guess we both know a thing or two about broken dreams," she said.

"I guess we do," he agreed.

"Thirty eight's not too old to start over, Cal," she said after a moment of heavy silence.

"Neither is thirty, Bailey," he added. "Maybe someday we'll both learn a thing or two about trying again."

"Maybe so," she said, and they finished the ride in quiet.

CHAPTER 9

"On Sundays we rest," Cal informed Bailey when she woke dressed to work.

"Oh," she said, not knowing how else to respond.

"The nature of the ranch is that it doesn't keep regular hours. I could pour my entire life into it, given the chance. It's an easy trap for me to fall into. I've found I'm more productive if I purpose a day of rest, to reflect, to refuel," he explained.

"Yes, sir," she said. She sat at the table and resisted the urge to drum her fingers. "I don't do well with inactivity."

"I sensed that about you. I used to be the same, but life has a way of catching up with you, little bit. What would you like for breakfast? It's Estralita's day off, too."

"Cereal is fine," she insisted.

"I don't do cereal, darlin'. It's either eggs and toast or waffles and bacon," he said.

"You…cook?" she said the word as if it were foreign. And it was, at least applied to him.

"Men can cook, Bailey. We can do anything women can do," he said, and she laughed because he was clearly making fun of her by putting on an affronted tone.

"That's not how I actually sound, is it?" she asked.

"You sound just fine," he said.

"What can I do to help?" she asked.

"Don't get in my way," he said.

"No one sits still and does nothing as well as I do," she said, perching on a high stool at the bar. A second later she had retrieved her notebook and began making notes. She wasn't aware Cal had noticed until he laid his hand on the notebook in front of her.

"No work today."

"You're killing me, here," she said.

"Why don't you set the table?" he asked. She hopped eagerly off the stool and set the table the same as Estralita did when they were having company—formally, with a knife, fork, spoon, napkin and two glasses in perfect alignment, one for juice and one for water.

"You set a fancy table, Major Dunbar," he commented.

"We lived in some remote places growing up. My mother insisted on adhering to civility. It was all she had because, as you can imagine, we were rather wild. 'Heathens' was her favorite word for us. We spent our days swinging from trees like the monkeys and snakes we tried to catch. But at supper we cleaned the dirt from under our nails and sat with our feet on the floor and our napkins in our laps like proper ladies."

"Sounds like you had the best of both worlds," he noted.

"Yes, sir," she agreed, her tone heavy with fondness and nostalgia.

"It might not surprise you to know I grew up much the same. Cam and I were rough and ready boys, anxious to prove ourselves as heirs to the estate. But our mother insisted on proper manners indoors. No spitting, no cursing, no hats at the table, wear a proper shirt and pants, and always use please and thank you and ma'am and sir."

"I like that," Bailey said.

"I do, too," Cal agreed, but his face looked a bit pinched. He thought he would have a crazy, busy houseful of children by now. The contrast of where he wanted to be and the still silence of his house was a painful reminder of how far off track his life had become.

"Is there anything else I can do?" Bailey asked before he could sink too far.

"I think that about does it," he said.

"Am I allowed to play the piano on Sundays?" she asked.

He opened his mouth and closed it again, amending what he was about to say. "I'm going to skip over the part where I'm surprised you can play the piano and try to embrace the fact that there are no limits to what you can do. I would love to hear you play the piano."

"I'm rusty," she warned.

"Now's the perfect chance to change that," he said, waving his spoon toward the formal living room where the piano was housed. A moment later songs began to drift out to him, some he recognized and some he didn't. His mom used to play and still did whenever she happened by the house. Hearing the sound now filled him with his own nostalgic longing. The ranch had been such a happy place once, before. And it also gave him a bit of hope. Maybe it could be so again. Bailey was right—he wasn't dead yet.

It would be worth any amount of money to get rid of Isabel, to let go of the weight of something that had been dragging him down for far too long. He had tried, earnestly tried to make things work. Even after she cheated on him he had tried to make it work. He had wanted to go to counseling, had gone so far as to make an appointment but, like always, Isabel ground her heels and said no. She had wanted it both ways, to have her fun on the side and keep him hanging on while paying the bills. For a while that had been okay because Cal was too deeply hurt, too wounded to do anything more than hang on and hope for the best. But his marriage was over and had been for a long time. It was irrevocably broken with no hope for salvation. Maybe at long last he could finally begin to let go. And to do that, he'd have to tell his family, to call his parents and his brother, swallow his ego and pride, and admit how badly he'd failed. He glanced at the phone. *Not today, but soon.*

A piano was one more thing Bailey loved and didn't own. She had taken lessons as a child, thanks to her mother's insistence her children have some culture. Bailey had taken to it with far more ease and devotion than either of her sisters. She had enjoyed being able to make ordinary black notes on a page come alive and turn into something beautiful. But like everything in her life, it had taken a back seat to her career.

Playing soothed her, and she wondered why she didn't do it more often. It wasn't that owning a piano was expensive—she often saw them for free or cheap. But she moved so often it would have been a nightmare to lug around.

She was so lost in the music it came as something of a surprise when Cal sat on the bench beside her. She jumped, startled, and her hands stilled on the keys.

"Don't stop on my account, I enjoy it," he said sincerely.

"I didn't hear you approach."

"You can thank my coach for that. Soft feet," he said, tossing her a wink.

"Do you play?" she asked.

"I know exactly one song," he said. He set his fingers on the keys and began playing the bass part of "Heart and Soul." Bailey joined in, playing the top part a few times until he nudged her with his elbow. "Breakfast is ready." She followed him to the kitchen and saw the table loaded with a heaping plate of bacon and a hearty stack of waffles.

"Exactly how many people are you expecting?" she asked.

"I've seen you eat. I think we'll be okay," he said.

She laughed, and he smiled. Isabel was always watching her weight, counting calories, and cutting out life's best tasting foods. Cal had spent most of their lives together eating alone while she picked at rabbit food. It was nice to be with someone who ate freely, who appreciated a good meal.

"Is this real maple syrup?" she asked.

"Yes. A colleague in Montana sends some every Christmas."

"What do you send him?" she asked.

"Humidity," he replied, and she laughed again.

They finished breakfast and cleaned up. It had been a pleasant morning, but Bailey saw the day yawning before her, an endless chasm of nothing.

"Would you like to take a ride with me?" Cal asked.

"Do you mean a tour from the owner himself?" she asked.

"I only do it for the really VIP guests," he said.

"You know I'm not a guest," she said. "I'm an, what's the word, employee."

"It doesn't feel that way to me, Bailey. It feels like you're an honored guest who's come to consult on ranch business."

"That's nice and all, but I'm still getting paid, right?" she joked.

"Why would you need money when you have all this?" he asked, spreading his hands wide to encompass the ranch.

"There's more truth in that than you know," she said, surveying the ranch as she sat atop her horse beside him. "I've missed this, being out away from people and back to the land. It does feel a bit like a vacation."

"Do you always tote a gun on vacation?" he asked, tapping the rifle strapped to her back.

"You could have stopped at 'do you always tote a gun' and the answer would still be yes. I always carry, always."

"You must have a fascinating dating life," he said, and she laughed.

"I had to draw a gun on a date once. He wasn't interested in taking no for an answer," she said.

"Did you shoot him?" Cal asked, his tone hopeful.

"Sadly, no. He had the idea I was joking, that he could wrestle the gun away from me and the fun would continue."

"What did you do?" he asked.

"I called my dad, the only time in my entire life I've resorted to the Daddy card."

"What happened?"

"I don't actually know, but I never saw the guy again. He wasn't at school on Monday, and his room had been cleaned out."

Cal whistled. "That's fatherhood done right."

"Yes, sir," she agreed.

"Stop calling me sir," he said.

"Yes, sir."

"You're testing my patience, little bit," he said.

"I imagine so, sir," she replied unconcernedly. "Where are you taking me?"

"To my favorite spot. You can swim, right? What am I saying, you went to the Naval Academy where they likely tried to drown you."

"Yes, sir," she agreed, and he smiled.

"Can I tell you a secret, Bailey?"

"Yes, sir."

"Growing up, I was a bit of a golden child. I was six years older than my brother, taller, a slightly better athlete, went pro at football, married a beauty queen. But I'm a bit jealous of him and his life. I wish I had gone the same route before settling back down to my roots. I wish I had been a soldier."

They reached the spot in question, a pond in the midst of dry, flat lands. He held out a hand to help her down off her horse and retained it so she could keep her balance while she took off her guns and holsters. He would have let go, but she held on to it a few beats, squeezing his hand as she spoke. "I've been a soldier a lot of years. I'm the daughter of a soldier, and here's what I've learned, Cal. Sometimes marines are made through training and experience and sometimes they're born already equipped with honor, integrity, loyalty, bravery, goodness, and every other thing we espouse. You fall into that second category. Your brother might have the training, but that's all you lack."

"That's a very sweet thing to say, little bit." He picked her up and tossed her headlong into the pond beside them.

"I was not ready for that," she said, surfacing like a half-drowned kitten.

"I thought your motto was always be prepared," he said, standing at the water's edge with hands on hips.

"I have a new motto, one based on retaliation. Come closer and I'll tell you in more detail," she said.

"With an offer like that, how can I resist?" He backed up a few steps, ran at the water and did a long range cannonball beside her. When he surfaced, she was nowhere to be seen, and then his knees gave way as she pushed them from behind, forcing him to collapse like a too-tall house of cards. He ducked under the water and reached for her, but she was a slippery eel, gliding around him like the Navy fish she was.

He thought he had her once, but she surfaced ten feet away. "There aren't alligators here, are there?" she called.

"Nah, they hang out in the eastern part of the state," he rejoined. "Don't tell me there's actually something you're afraid of. They're just harmless reptiles."

"I'll put one in the plane, take you up for a spin, and see how it goes," she offered.

"Anyone ever told you you're a brat?" he asked, flicking a heavy splash of water in her direction.

"Yes, sir," she replied.

"Come over here, let me tell you more," he said.

"I'm staying over here for your benefit, sir. Swimming is the best exercise for the elderly."

"All right, that's it," he said and disappeared beneath the water. After a while longer of chasing, he finally caught her. They emerged from the water, his right arm around her waist. With his left, he pushed the wet hair off her face. The atmosphere morphed immediately from lighthearted fun to expectant and tense. Cal dropped his arms and swam back a pace, allowing the water to come between them.

"We should probably get back," he said.

"Yes, sir," she agreed and ducked beneath the water, putting a few yards of distance between them.

He stayed where he was until she emerged onto the bank and refastened her holsters. Then it was his turn to haul himself out. He shook his hair like a dog, slid his hat on, and swung into the saddle.

They rode home in silence. It wasn't an uncomfortable silence, but it was a tiny bit sad, and neither wanted to put a name to why. "Thank you for that, Cal. It was a fun day," Bailey said when they returned to the stable. "I'm going to go get cleaned up after I help with the horses."

"I'll take care of the horses," he offered, reaching for her reins. She handed them over, being careful not to let their fingers brush.

He stayed in the barn for a long time, until long after the horses were brushed and fed and watered. The barn worked the same soothing magic on him as usual so that by the time he went inside his equilibrium was restored. He took a shower and prepped some steaks while Bailey scrubbed and prepared potatoes for baking.

They ate supper, talking and laughing like old friends, keeping things casual and light. After supper was finished and cleaned up, they retired to the porch with a glass of tea, one shared between them as had become their custom since she first arrived. Instead of sitting in separate rockers like usual, Cal sat on the loveseat glider, stretching his arm over the back of it. Bailey sat beside him, keeping a safe distance away, her legs tucked beneath her.

His long legs rocked them gently for a while as they sat in easy silence, enjoying the tropically humid, quiet night. Eventually he realized she was asleep. Her lolling head crept closer and closer to him until it landed on his shoulder. He closed his eyes and fought a wave of longing so intense it became painful to breathe. He wanted more than the life he had now, wanted more than an estranged wife who hated him so much she flaunted a string of boyfriends to torment him, wanted to be whole and healthy again. Mostly he wanted Bailey. She was so close, and yet so far out of reach. He couldn't, wouldn't break his vows. As long as he was still married, they still meant something to him. And it would be wholly unfair to drag her into the tangled mess his world had become. She would be one more innocent victim of a mistake he made a decade ago that was still causing harm.

But his fingers refused to accept the message his brain sent. They stole closer, his thumb easing along her shoulder. The light touch woke her. She sat up, blinking at him in confusion.

"You fell asleep," he whispered.

"Sorry," she replied, also in a whisper. Her eyes roamed his face, and his heart squeezed and turned over. It was both a hope and a curse to have her look at him that way. On the one hand, his attraction to her wasn't one sided. On the other hand, it needed to remain so.

"Bailey," he began, his tone strangled with repressed emotion.

"I know," she said. She straightened and sat up away from him. "Nice night," she added, surveying the darkened landscape. He didn't respond because he couldn't. If he opened his mouth, he was afraid of what might come out. After another moment, she stood. "Goodnight, sir."

His continued silence probably seemed rude, but he was certain she understood. He remained on the porch a long time after she went to bed, letting the night's peace wash over him and soothe him with its usual magic.

CHAPTER 10

On Monday Bailey began implementing the new security changes around the ranch. The hands would vary their routines and keep a log of any suspicious vehicles. These she would report to law enforcement and hope something got done about them. She posted signs all over the problem areas, both in English and in Spanish, stating the area was under observation and air patrol and violators would be turned in. This she hoped might be enough to stem the flow of cow thefts by people looking to make a quick, easy buck.

In the south pasture, where the smugglers were wearing an even bigger path, she instituted a bit of road reconstruction, adding piles of gravel as speed bumps, along with some well-placed rocks and boulders. The hands who used the road would know about the new construction. The smugglers who used it in the dead of night would not, or so Bailey hoped. While not ready to wage an all-out war with them, she wanted to make them feel as unwelcome as possible, sending a subtle signal to go away.

The other change that took place was the relationship between Bailey and Cal. It was as if they had both decided to withdraw from each other, albeit politely. They were still polite to each other, but there was a new and cool reserve between them when before they had been well on their way to becoming good friends. Each of them knew, but neither of them said, there was no way they could remain on their current trajectory without some sort of cataclysmic ending neither of them could handle.

For her part, her goal remained lowering her blood pressure enough to return to the marines. Having a romance with a married rancher did not figure into that plan. For his part, he was unwilling and unable to enter into any sort of dalliance while still married. And he was still very much married, a fact he was painfully reminded of when he cut a check to Isabel for ten thousand dollars. It was a worrisome amount of money, even for her, and he began to wonder why she needed or wanted so much. Was he also outfitting her boyfriend's lifestyle? He told himself he wouldn't stand for that, but really he had no idea what he would take anymore. A long time ago he said he would never stay with a woman who was unfaithful to him, and here he was, two years later and still in her clutches.

Isabel arrived to pick up her check as Bailey returned from an air patrol. She exited the plane and saw the other woman on her horse, practicing her barrel races. It surprised her because Isabel looked like the kind of woman who would keep her distance from any animal, but horse love knew no boundaries. She paused, standing by Jinx to watch the other woman ride, winding her horse expertly through the course.

"Dang woman showed up in the middle of the workday and demanded I saddle her mount like she's still queen of the castle," Jinx muttered. His horse stood patiently by, as did the one Bailey had been using. "Thought you might want it when you got back," he added.

"Thank you," she said, linking her arm with his and giving it a squeeze. She had grown ridiculously fond of the old man in her short time on the ranch. They got each other in a way that didn't need words. *Sympathetic hearts,* her mother would say. It was the same with…but, no, she wouldn't allow herself to think of him. He wasn't hers. He belonged to the woman in front of her, the one whose horse looked as weary of her as everyone else.

Isabel finished her ride and stopped short beside them, tossing her reins to Jinx. "Well, it's cute little Bailey. How's life with my husband? He treating you all right?"

Bailey swallowed a thousand replies, answering only with a cool stare. There was something off about the woman, something she couldn't quite place, more than her nasty demeanor. Bailey was distrustful of her, almost leery. She was the sort you didn't want to turn your back on, for certain.

"Do you ride?" Isabel tried again, her curled lip telling her no answer from Bailey would be satisfactory.

"Not as much as I'd like," Bailey said.

"For a hot minute, I thought of competing this year at the fair. And then I thought, 'I was Miss America. Is this what my life has become now? Racing barrels at the county fair?'" She huffed a disdainful, humorless laugh and Bailey felt a moment of pity for her. Not because she had fallen so far but because she had perfection at her fingertips and hadn't realized.

Isabel, an astute observer of people and especially other women, read the look for what it was and hated her even more for it. "Let me give you some advice, little girl. You go back to where you came from while you still can, before this place latches onto you and kills that little spark that keeps you young and vibrant. This is no place for a fresh, innocent thing like you. And my husband is not up for grabs." For emphasis, she reached out and gave Bailey a hard shove in the chest.

Jinx stepped forward, "Miss Isabel, enough," he said in a warning tone.

"Shut up, you old fool. You know Cal keeps you around out of pity because he's too soft to let you go. That's going to change when I'm in control of the ranch."

"You'll get control of this ranch over Cal's dead body," Jinx said.

"That can be arranged much easier than you think," Isabel said.

Bailey reached for her horse and began to unsaddle it. They watched as she then unlaced her boots and took off her socks. "I think I will go for a ride, Jinx. Thank you for getting my horse for me." To Isabel she added. "I'm in charge of security on the ranch now.

Threaten my boss again, and I'll bury you so deep they'll never find the body. Now watch how we do it in Africa." She swung up onto her horse, barefoot and bareback, threading her fingers through its mane. She kneed it gently, and it took off at top speed. She raced easily through the barrels, jumped the fence at the other side, and kept going.

"She sure can ride," Jinx said, knowing it was the exact thing that would rile Isabel the most.

"Take my horse and bring the car," Isabel demanded.

"I'll take the horse 'cause you don't treat him right, but you get your own car. I don't work for you." He took the horses and turned away, leaving her fuming in frustration and anger.

The next morning Bailey patrolled the south pasture in a truck. It was the first morning after the new road construction, and she wanted to see if it had any effect.

It was early morning, the sun barely up, so she had to squint to make sure she saw what she saw. Another truck sat on the gravel path the smugglers used, apparently disabled. Two men stood outside it, staring at it in obvious frustration. Bailey stepped from the truck and peered at them through binoculars. Judging by the men's arm and face tattoos, they appeared to be part of the local gang she had studied and read up on. They were known to be a brutal, ruthless regime, killing anyone who crossed them. Bailey's attention turned to their truck and she couldn't hold back a chuckle of amusement. They had hit one of the new speed bumps, probably at top speed, and broken their front axle.

"Take that, and now go away," she whispered.

Of course they were too far away to hear her, but they could clearly see her truck, see her standing beside it with binoculars. One of them raised a gun and shot in her direction. He went far wide of where she stood, but Bailey dove behind the truck anyway. The type of gun he used could easily chew through the metal of the truck's doors. She positioned herself behind the engine, the only thing that could stop a bullet of that caliber.

The next shot blew out the driver's side window. Bailey raised her rifle, trained it on the first man's head, and then dropped it, systematically shooting out all four of their tires. When their guns remained lowered, she knew they'd been testing her, seeing how she would respond.

She opened the passenger side door, slid inside, started the car and drove backwards away from them. When she was a safe enough distance away, she turned the truck around and drove back toward the ranch.

What next? she wondered. It would be something, she knew, but what she couldn't say. She would need to be prepared for anything; they all would.

It was her bad luck Cal was outside when she got back to the ranch. "What happened?" he asked, coming to stand beside the missing window of his truck.

"Our smuggler friends and I exchanged some gunfire," she said.

"What?" He opened the door, put up a hand, and pulled her out to stand in front of him. "Are you okay?" His eyes scanned her for any possible signs of injury.

"They're not good shots," she informed him. "This was a fluke." She tapped the door. "They were aiming for the tires. So I returned the favor and shot out their tires."

"You shot out their tires?" he said.

"Yes, but that's nothing compared to their broken axle. I'd say they're going to need a new truck."

He leaned on the truck as the air whooshed out of him. "Bailey, this is bad."

"It's not so bad," she said, mimicking his pose and leaning beside him.

"No, it's bad. They don't quit. There is no such thing as de-escalation with them. It's going to grow and grow until someone is hurt or killed."

"It's going to grow until someone ends it, once and for all," she said.

"What are you saying?" he asked.

"I'm saying at some point they're going to become more than an annoyance. At some point they're going to need to be stopped."

"Border patrol won't do it," he said.

"I wasn't talking about them," she said.

"What are you going to do, sneak over to Mexico and kill them all?"

She shrugged.

He faced her. "Bailey, you can't do that."

"Why not?"

"Because it's illegal."

"So is what they're doing," she said.

"But it's murder."

"It's war, Cal. It's not always black and white."

"It's not…" he swallowed hard. "I don't want that. I don't want anyone getting hurt."

"Then I'll respect your wishes. For now. But it was inevitable someone was going to take the first shot. Let the record show it was them. Excuse me, I have to clean my gun." She shouldered her rifle and turned to go.

He watched her walk away, dread and respect comingling inside him. What if something happened to her because he'd brought her here to help? How would he live with it if she was wounded or, worse, killed? He couldn't live with that. But what could he do? She wouldn't back away now that she'd gotten started. She would see things through to the end, whatever end that might be.

He closed his eyes and thought of her streaking across the ranch, bareback and barefoot. He had made himself scarce when Isabel arrived, not wanting another confrontation. But he had been nearby keeping a wary eye on her, never trusting her completely anymore. He had watched Bailey one up her on her horse before jumping the fence and taking off. And it had taken everything in his power not to swing onto his own horse and follow. He felt as if he were on a precipice, trying to keep watch on too many things that could spiral disastrously out of control—Bailey, Isabel, the ranch. He was weary and, worse, he was in charge, so he pulled out his phone and called someone about the truck. It was one small thing, but he felt better after it was taken care of. Maybe that was the key, to take one small step at a time until the marathon was over.

CHAPTER 11

The next day Bailey returned from her mid-morning patrol and heard shouting. She hurried forward and saw a group of about fifteen boys standing in the yard with Cal, shouting at him in Spanish. Cal stood out like a maypole, several feet taller than all the boys. In his hands was a football.

Bailey set down her pack. "Room for one more?"

"What do you think, boys, should we let her play? *Deberíamos dejarla jugar?*"

About half the boys shouted yes while the other half shouted no. "Looks like our teams just divided themselves," Bailey said, holding her hands aloft. Cal threw her the ball, and she easily caught it, impressing the boys who had aligned themselves with her.

"I think you have a new fan club," Cal said. "Let me know if you need me to translate."

"I've got it, thanks," she said, gathering the boys around her and making plans with them in fluent Spanish.

Cal rolled his eyes. Was there anything the woman couldn't do? A new thought occurred to him, some way he thought he could outdo her. "Bailey, can you cook?"

"Wait until you try my paella," she said, smiling, and he got caught up staring at her for a few seconds until the boys around him began to bump and jostle for his attention.

The game was intensely competitive. Cal started out as he always did, going soft in order to teach, to coach. But Bailey was having none of it. She was out for blood, and he soon caught her mania, playing rough and dirty and doing whatever it took to win, short of hurting anyone. There he had to be careful. The boys were rough and tumble but so much smaller than him he felt like Gulliver among the Lilliputians. But every time he took a dive in order not to jeopardize anyone's safety, Bailey taunted him for it, as if it hadn't been on purpose, as if he actually were getting too old and out of shape to play the game. Eventually his mood turned from amusement to irritation. He could only be pushed so far before he would retaliate, and she finally pushed the button enough times that he forgot himself completely and tackled her, burying her hard beneath him.

The air whooshed out of her in a rush and he had immediate regrets.

"I'm sorry," he apologized, easing slightly away from her to make sure she was still conscious and breathing.

She held up a hand and shook her head. "Fine," she whispered. Her eyes were filled with tears of pain, and he felt like a total heel.

"No, I'm really sorry. Sometimes I get so competitive I forget my own strength."

"My fault," she said, taking a deeper breath.

"How is it your fault I tackled you?" he asked.

"I goaded you into it," she said.

He shook his head. "I shouldn't have."

"It was what I wanted. You fell into my trap," she said.

"You're smashed on the ground beneath me, and you think I'm the one in a trap?" he asked, clearly not buying what she was selling.

She grinned up at him, nodding. "While you were distracted clobbering me, we finished the play, made a touchdown and won the game."

Finally he realized the boys behind him were not yelling because they were upset but because they were amused and delighted. It was exactly as she said—she tricked and manipulated him, distracting him so easily with taunts that he allowed them to walk away with a victory.

"You little minx," he said, half irritated and half amused again.

"For the record, sir, I have no idea what that old timey word means. Also, you're actually beginning to crush me and I can no longer breathe."

"Give me a minute, I think I broke something when I fell," he said.

"What?" she asked, her tone morphing to immediate concern.

"My resolve," he said. His eyes fell to her lips. "Bailey, I want..."

"Don't, Cal, *don't*. They're all watching us, and you'll hate yourself after, you know you will."

"What would I do without you here to save me from myself?" he asked.

"I think if I weren't here you wouldn't be having the problem in the first place," she said. "Now get off me, you big galoot."

"You think minx is archaic, and you say things like galoot?" he said. He rolled off her and put a hand down to pull her up.

A pickup truck pulled up in the yard, grabbing their attention.

"Here we go," Cal said, dropping Bailey's hand.

"Cal, Major Dunbar, boys," Sully said, tipping his hat to them.

"Sully," Cal returned while Bailey remained silent.

"*Hola*, Ranger Langford," the boys chorused.

"Looks like I missed the fun." Sully's eyes roamed the group, pausing on a disheveled, dirt-smeared Bailey. She steeled herself, waiting for his inevitable commentary or disbelief.

"Who won?" he said instead.

"We did," Bailey replied.

"Because you cheated. Again," Cal said.

"Bitterness is a bad color on you, sir," Bailey replied, and he flicked her ponytail.

"I wanted to come by and check on y'all, see how it's going," Sully continued.

"It's fine," Bailey volunteered, letting Cal know she wouldn't be volunteering information about her shootout with the smugglers.

"Very well, I also felt the need to pass something along. Seeing as how you no longer attend town dances, Cal, I thought you might not have mentioned the one this Friday to Bailey," Sully said. His eyes landed on Bailey, raising slightly at the dirt smears on her face. "Though now that I'm taking a second look, I see that might be useless information for a woman who prefers football and shooting. You are clearly not a dancer. Sorry, disregard."

"I enjoy dancing a lot, actually," Bailey said, and now Sully's eyes rose with surprise.

"You do?"

"Yes," Bailey said.

"Would you like to prove it on Friday?" he asked.

"I..." she froze, realizing he'd bested and trapped her. She sighed, resigned. "Fine."

"That's the spirit, Major. I'll pick you up at seven. You don't have to wear a dress, but I'd clean the mud off your face a bit."

"I'll go do that now," she said, escaping inside before he tricked her into dinner with him.

"Looks like you did your homework," Cal commented.

"You gotta know your audience, Cal," Sully agreed, tipping his hat. "That's my new and improved A-game, by the way."

"Best of luck to you and yours," Cal said, tossing the football up in the air and catching it handily a few times.

"You worried?" Sully asked.

"Do I look it?" Cal asked. "Dances are a young man's game."

"What's an old man's game?"

"When I figure it out, I'll let you know," Cal promised.

"I used to watch you play ball when I was a kid, Cal. Some of my earliest memories are watching you tear it up on the field. You were something else." He motioned to the group of boys standing behind him. "I gotta say, I like you better now." He held his hands up for the ball.

"Me, too," Cal agreed, lobbing him an easy pass.

"Are we okay?" Sully asked, tossing it back.

Cal caught the ball and turned his hand to show Sully his ring. "I've still got this, don't I?" He tossed the ball back.

"And when you don't, what happens then?" Sully asked, catching the ball and tossing it back.

"I can hardly imagine," Cal said.

Sully caught the ball and held it, scanning the horizon before he spoke. "You be careful, Cal. Isabel is…things aren't good."

"I can handle Isabel. I've been doing it the last ten years," Cal said.

"This time's different. It's a bad time to get a guard girl," he said.

"Bailey can handle herself," Cal assured him.

"Maybe she can handle herself in a war with a platoon of men backing her up, but this is Texas. She's all alone and rules don't apply," Sully said, finally tossing the ball.

Cal handed it off to the group of boys behind him, indicating with a nod of his head for them to run off. Two of them were Estralita's grandsons. The others he wasn't exactly certain where they came from or how much English they understood. They were nice kids, but without knowing who their relatives were, he couldn't trust them completely.

"I trust Bailey. If I didn't, I wouldn't keep her here."

"You sure that's why you're keeping her here, Cal? Because of trust?" Sully pressed.

"Why else, Sullivan?"

"Can't think of a reason, Calhoun. See y'all Friday."

Cal crossed his arms over his chest and watched him drive away, a vague sense of foreboding filling his chest. He felt Sully had been trying to warn him about something, but what? Or, as with rams, had it been merely the jousting of two males over the attention of an eligible female? He'd been away from the game so long it was hard to tell.

He turned toward the house and felt the telltale pain of a strained muscle in his hip. Reluctantly he admitted he had put a bit too much of himself into the game, not only because he wanted to win but because he wanted to impress Bailey. And now he paid the price, proving it was possible to be old in body and young in stupidity. On the other hand, it was good to know despite his age, some things remained the same. Once stupid for women, always stupid for women; the consistency was heartening.

CHAPTER 12

Two days later, Bailey received a package.

"You get more ammo?" Jinx asked. In addition to changing up their routine, she had instituted a policy that sent cowboys in pairs when they had to go to the south pasture. She also added target practice to their daily routine. The men were fair shots, but their guns were hardly used, only to frighten away the occasional mountain lion or coyote intent on poaching a calf. Last year Jinx's son, Corrie, shot a rattler, and it was still a topic of great interest for the men as there was some debate over how close he'd come to shooting out the toes of his brother, Jonah.

"No," Bailey said, not bothering to explain as she knelt and cut open the box. She unfurled a dress and held it aloft before stuffing it quickly back into the box and removing a pair of shoes. Then she held onto Jinx's arm for balance while she whipped off her combat boots and socks before slipping into the new shoes.

"If this is some kind of new uniform, the men ain't going to be happy," he said.

"Not breaking in new shoes before a dance is a rookie move," she said and then took Jonah's rifle, checked the sight he complained was misaligned, and shot through the heart of his target.

"Sight's fine, it's your aim that's off," she told him, patting his back to soften the blow.

She finished the rest of the day in the new shoes, and it was a testament to how well the men were beginning to know her that no one thought twice about it. In fact no one seemed to notice them much at all besides Cal who did a double take at supper.

"Those for the dance?" he guessed.

"Yes, sir."

"So you are planning to wear a dress," he said.

"It's a dance, sir," she returned.

"Huh."

"Is there a problem?" she asked.

"No. I'm sure Sully will be thrilled with the transformation." He took a bite of his stew, chewed and swallowed. "I have to say I was a little surprised he roped you so easily into the dance."

She shrugged.

"He didn't exactly trick you, did he?"

"I spend a lot of time in a man's world. Sometimes it's nice to put on a dress and remember I'm a woman," she said.

"Strange, I'd be hard pressed to forget it," he replied.

They shared a smile until she finally dropped her eyes to her stew.

On the day of the dance, she worked like usual. She and Cal ate supper together and then she disappeared while he retired to the porch with a glass of tea.

Sully arrived in his personal vehicle instead of his work truck so basically he had traded the white pickup for the red one. He wore khaki pants and a button down shirt and his ubiquitous white hat.

"You look good enough for church," Cal called.

"Thanks, but I already have a date," Sully returned. "Where is she?"

"Dunno, haven't seen her in a bit," Cal said.

"I'm here," Bailey said, appearing in the doorway.

Neither man replied because neither could. For a few beats, they were rendered speechless. Since her arrival she had worn some variation of jeans and a t-shirt with her hair in its tidy ponytail, her face free of makeup. Now she wore a gray dress, fitted at the waist and flaring to her knees, the spaghetti straps up top showcasing her tanned, toned shoulders and arms. Her hair hung in soft waves and she wore enough makeup to highlight her eyes and lips.

"Goodnight, Cal," she said softly, alerting him to the fact he was staring.

"Goodnight, little bit." He should probably tell her to have fun, but he couldn't make the words emerge.

She faced forward, toward Sully. "Am I allowed to tell you how good you look?" he asked.

"No," she returned.

"All right then," he said. He opened her door and took her hand to help her up, closing the door when she was safely inside. He tipped his hat to Cal, jogged to his side of the car, and took off.

They drove a few minutes in silence until he spoke. "I feel I owe you an apology." When she didn't reply, he continued. "No response?"

"It seems ungracious to agree with that statement," she said.

"When women show up in my office, they're usually either crackpots or something altogether different."

"Predatory," she guessed.

"It seems ungracious to agree with that statement," he said and she laughed. "I admit I didn't quite know what to make of you, and you caught me off guard. Since then I've done some checking on you, and you're the real deal, Major Dunbar. I apologize that I acted so rudely and unprofessionally."

"Apology accepted, Ranger Langford, thank you," she said, relaxing a bit. Maybe he was a normal guy after all. And he wasn't too shabby to look at either, with sandy blond hair and eyes that were neither green nor blue but somewhere in between. Not like Cal with his devilishly dark hair and eyes.

"Why did you leave the marines?" he asked.

"High blood pressure."

He clicked his tongue in sympathy. "What do you have planned after you leave here?"

"I'll probably take a nice, long bath, get the dust and humidity off me, and then I have no idea," she said, turning to gaze out the window.

"Uh oh, I've bumbled into negative territory. I'm sure you'll figure something out."

"What would you do, if you had to leave the rangers?" she asked.

He opened his mouth, closed it, and shook his head.

"Exactly."

"It's different for women though, isn't it?" he asked.

"Haven't we been over this?" she said.

"Don't you want kids?" he asked.

"Lots of women have kids in the military," she said.

"Lots of women like you? Whose jobs demand physical performance and the high likelihood of not returning home again? I mean, say you'd stayed in, wouldn't you have had to come to some kind of crisis moment anyway? Would you really want to stay in and have to sit behind a desk?"

She grimaced.

"I'm not saying it's an easy thing for you, don't get me wrong. What I'm saying is maybe it's a blessing in disguise. A chance to take the reins of change before they're forced on you. This way you won't have to resent some man for getting you pregnant and thereby forcing you out of a career you love. Your own body already did it for you."

She stared at him, eyes narrowed. "I'm not sure if that's sexist or brilliant."

He tapped his temple. "There's a lot going on under the hat, and I have a lot of time to think about things, driving around in my truck."

"Yours must be an interesting job," she noted, ready to change the subject away from herself. "How'd you come to be a ranger?"

"A long shot dream and a lot of hard work," he said.

It came as something of a surprise to Bailey when they arrived in town. The drive had seemed short, the conversation with Sully enjoyable. She began to believe her initial impression of him had been incorrect. He wasn't a self-important moron after all.

Sully introduced her to several people in the town who all seemed to know her already. "Oh, Cal's girl. You clean up nice. Where is Cal?" she was asked so many times the faces and voices began to blur.

Finally enough people were on the dance floor it wouldn't be awkward to join them. Sully led Bailey onto the floor for a line dance that proved to be fun, once she got the hang of it. The dancing was mostly either line or contra, fast and in groups that left little chance for touching or conversation. Every once in a while they threw in a waltz. Bailey found to her further surprise she didn't mind dancing these with Sully, either. He was a good dancer, and he never held her too closely or pressed her for more than she was willing to give.

"You really do clean up nice," he said during one such dance.

"I'd say you do, too, but I've never seen you messy," she said.

"See that kind of sounds like a put down coming from you," he said.

"It's not, I promise."

"I don't know you well enough to know what a promise is worth," he said.

"I'm a marine; it's worth everything," she said.

"Are you flirting with me?" he asked.

"About as much as you're flirting with me, never more," she said.

"Well then I'm definitely going to have to step it up," he said.

"I can't promise I'll follow suit," she said.

"A chance I'm willing to take," he said, easing her a tiny bit closer.

When that dance ended, they paused to grab something to drink. Sully ran into someone else he knew and became ensnared in a conversation. After the initial greeting, Bailey stood beside him, bored and trying not to show it. It was hard for her to relax, even at a dance. So when the environment of the room shifted, she noticed. She straightened and turned, expecting to see danger. What she saw instead was Calhoun Ridge, tall, dark, foreboding, and impossibly handsome, wearing a suit and making his way toward her. She told herself to turn around, to look away, but she couldn't. She remained rooted to the spot, staring at him as he stared at her, easing closer and closer, winding his way through bodies until at last he was right beside her. He clasped her hand.

"Sully, you mind if I have this dance?"

"I'll say yes, seeing as how I don't seem to have much of a choice," Sully replied.

A waltz began to play. Bailey had the suspicion it was on purpose, as if whoever controlled the music was doing them a favor. Cal was a good dancer, and he made no pretense of keeping a space between them, as Sully had done. He tucked her close and clasped her hand, resting it on his chest between them.

"Thought you weren't coming," she said.

"Sully rightfully pointed out I haven't been to one of these in a while. I don't want people getting the mistaken impression I'm stand-offish," he said.

"I don't think anyone watching you right now would think that," she said.

"Plus I needed to tell you somethin' and ask you somethin'."

"Go on," she urged.

"You're beautiful. You're beautiful when you're like this, and you're beautiful when you're not."

"Thank you," she said, the words a croaky whisper. They danced in silence a few beats before she spoke again. "What did you want to ask me?"

"Do you ever think you want to settle down and have children, Bailey?"

The question was so close to the conversation she'd had with Sully it felt eerie. "Yes."

"How many?"

"Four or five ought to do."

The corners of his mouth tugged slightly. "That ought to do just fine."

She glanced at his left hand, the one holding hers, and noted he still wore his ring. He followed the line of her gaze as the dance came to an end. "I should go."

"So that's it? You drove an hour to show up at a dance, tell me I'm beautiful, ask me about children, and drive away again?"

"I'm only human, Bailey, and I wanted one dance with you in that dress."

She stepped out of his embrace. "You've had it. Goodnight, Cal."

"Goodnight," he said. He lingered a few beats longer and then turned and walked away, out of the hall, into the moonless night.

Bailey waited until he was safely gone and turned the opposite direction. She found a door that led to the back alley and took it, stepping through and inhaling the heavy air. It was a close night, oppressively so. For a moment it felt hard to breathe. She leaned on the wall and tried to force air into her lungs.

The door beside her opened and closed and then someone leaned on the wall beside her. "You want to talk about it?" Sully offered.

"No, thank you," Bailey returned.

"You want to cry?" he asked almost hopefully.

"I'm not so good at crying," she said.

"Shame. I'm ridiculously good at comforting crying women," he said.

She laughed a bit. "I could guess that you are."

He took a deep breath and let it out. "As it seems any sort of romance between us is doomed before it gets off the ground, what do you say to being friends?"

"I'd say it sounds spectacular," she said, surprising him by linking her arm through his and giving it a squeeze.

"Good. As your friend, I have something to tell you, something worrisome and important. It's about Isabel."

Bailey tensed. "What about her?"

"Cal won't hear a word about who she's dating, but I think you need to know. She's been seeing the head of the cartel."

Bailey looked at him, stunned. "What?"

Sully blew out another breath and swiped his hand over his face. "Isabel has always been difficult, hard to like, standoffish and a snob. Why Cal married her, we'll never… Anyway, about a year ago I began to notice some changes in her, bigger mood swings, more erratic decision making. I became suspicious, so I started keeping an eye on her."

"Drugs?" Bailey guessed. That had been the missing thing she hadn't been able to put her finger on, the strange affect in Isabel's concerning behavior.

"Drugs," Sully confirmed "After she blew through all the money

Cal gave her, she began offering other things in exchange for them. Eventually that turned into some sort of relationship, such as it is. I mean, you've seen her. She's a beautiful woman, exactly the sort a drug kingpen would like to have in his keep."

"She threatened Cal. I thought it was all talk," Bailey said.

"It wasn't," Sully said.

They were silent a minute, each of them digesting the conversation. "What did you say when she said that?" he asked at last.

"I told her if she ever said it again, I'd kill her, and I meant it," she said.

He paused a few beats longer, staring at the far wall. "Do it in Mexico. I have no jurisdiction there."

He sounded half joking, but Bailey thought he was fully serious.

"I got in a shootout with some gang members. I took out their tires. Since then, I've been waiting for the other shoe to drop," she said.

"Girl, you know how to make friends, don't you?" he said.

"It's going to get worse before it gets better," she said.

"Their idea of worse might be far more than what you're thinking," he said.

"Then I'll have to make plenty sure my idea of the worst is more than they've ever dreamed," she said.

He blinked at her. "I can honestly say this is the most interesting date I've ever had."

"As dates go, it's not half bad." She clasped his hand and tugged him toward the door. "Let's dance more."

"Okay, and if anyone asks, Cal and I fought for you, and I won."

She smiled up at him. "The first rule of telling a lie is to keep it believable, Sully. Let's say you fought, and I beat you both."

"The longer I know you, the more believable that sounds," he said. He opened the door for her and allowed her to precede him inside.

CHAPTER 13

The next morning Bailey woke at dawn to go for a run, as was her normal routine. Unlike normal, Cal jogged up beside her and kept an easy pace at her side. They ran what she guessed to be about two miles and then turned back toward the house, still without speaking. About the last mile or so, she picked up her speed, and so did he. She pushed it harder, and he followed suit. They sprinted neck and neck until, the last hundred feet to the house, he overtook her, bounded up the steps, and touched the door first.

She joined him a few seconds later and doubled over, sucking oxygen. Cal lay flat on his back, doing the same.

"Can't win them all, little bit," he said.

"I'm leaving," she said, and he sat up.

"What?"

She stood upright. "Things are in good shape here. The men know better what to do, how to handle themselves. I've established a security plan for them, and they're more aware of the danger, as well as their surroundings. You have Sully if there's a problem or emergency. I think my work here is about done."

"What will you do?" he asked.

"Jinx's mom had one of those blood pressure cuffs he's been letting me borrow. I've been checking it every day, and it's been perfect. If I get it documented and verified by a doctor, I can go back. I can be a marine again."

He hugged his knees to his chest, wrapping his long arms around them. "I'm not ready for you to go."

She took his left hand, the one still wearing his ring. "Darlin', you're not ready for me to stay." She gave his hand a squeeze, bypassed him, and went to take a shower.

When she emerged, Cal was nowhere to be seen. Bailey put the coffee he'd left for her in a travel mug and hightailed it outside to avoid another encounter with him. She hopped in the plane and took off for her morning patrol. She followed her own advice, mixing up her patrols so she didn't keep the same routine each day. It took conscious effort because she was the sort of person who thrived on routine.

She had completed her first turn when she saw smoke rising from below. Wildfires were a real concern in such a dry, hot environment. Bailey circled once more and set the plane down, intending to investigate.

She withdrew the plane's fire extinguisher and stepped out into the blazing sunshine. Even wearing her sunglasses she had to shade her eyes in order to see anything. She scanned the horizon and saw nothing but a small brush fire, one that already tried to leap its confines and blaze out of control. She used the extinguisher on it, pouring foam on the surrounding area to try and dissuade any sparks from getting further ideas. When she was satisfied, she made as if to pivot back to the plane when suddenly an iron grip surrounded her from behind. A vice-like arm wrapped around her neck, cutting off her air.

"Let's have some fun," a man whispered in Spanish. From the hard feel of his chest, Bailey could tell he wore Kevlar. He was bigger than her, stronger, and wearing a bullet-proof vest. There was no way she could out-muscle him so she'd have to outfight him. She went slack, forcing him to take her full weight or drop her. He chose to take her weight, leaning in to get a better grip. As he bent forward, she reared her head back, bashing her skull into his face. It was enough to make him lose his grip on her completely.

She was little, lithe, and fast. Those would be her only advantages so she used them as best she could, spinning out of his grasp and reaching for the tactical stick on her belt. The Kevlar wasn't the only thing that kept her from reaching for the gun. His size was a factor. If he overpowered her, got the gun away from her, she'd have zero chance. Her best bet was to take him by surprise, to disable him before he was ready for it.

He lunged for her with his right hand but, like a lot of large men, he relied on his size and physique with no real idea how to use them. They would work well on someone who wasn't a trained fighter, who didn't know how to fight back. Lucky for Bailey she did.

She brought the stick down hard on his right forearm while shoving his wrist in the opposite direction. There was a satisfying crack of bone, and he screamed. For good measure, she broke a few of his fingers, disabling his dominant hand and arm completely.

He wore a helmet, she now saw, and it would need to come off. She bashed the butt of the stick into the center of his face. He screamed again as his nose and lip exploded with blood and ruined cartilage. He flailed at her blindly, his left hand connecting hard with her face. She felt her own lip split as her eye began to throb, but she ignored it, her fingers scrambling for the strap of his helmet as she yanked it off and tossed it away.

His hands went protectively to his head, afraid she was about to hit him there. Instead she reached for the vest, yanking hard at the Velcro until it pulled free. When that was finished, she brought the club up between his legs. He bent forward, retching, moaning, not sure what to cover next. Bailey connected the stick with his kneecap and shoved his back. He went down like a dead tree, lumbering to his stomach in a ungraceful heap. She sat on his back, reached for a ziptie from her pants and started to truss. He fought her. She clutched the stick and gave a glancing blow to his forehead, knocking him unconscious.

When he was out, she tied his hands and bound his feet. She stood, panting, scanning the horizon for more of his friends. For now, they were alone. She would have to haul him into the plane, and she was dangerously low on energy. Clutching his vest and helmet in one hand, she opened the plane's passenger door with the other. After setting the gear on the seat, she reached for her attacker and began hauling him unceremoniously into the cab of the plane.

He must have weighed close to two hundred pounds. There was no way to get him onto the seat, but then she didn't much care to. She dragged his torso onto the floor of the plane, hauled his feet onto the seat, and buckled them with the safety belt in case he came to and tried to kick her.

After giving the fire one last spray of foam, she tossed the empty canister back into the cockpit, hopped inside, and took off.

Cal waited for her when she landed. He opened the door and extended a hand to help her out. "We need to talk."

"Could you call Sully?" she asked. She was so tired now the words felt as if they were wrenched from somewhere deep and painful.

Cal tilted his head at her. "What's wrong?"

She motioned with her thumb to the plane behind her. He stuck his head inside and said a word that, though indiscernible to her, did not sound like a prayer of thanksgiving.

He withdrew his head and scanned her face, clutching it between his palms as he made his inspection. "What did he do to you?"

"Just this," she said, motioning to the busted lip and swollen eye.

"That's all?"

"That's all. Call Sully and I'll fill you in." He let go of her and she sank to the ground. He knelt beside her, alarmed.

"I'm fine, I swear. Just used up all my adrenaline and need to recover a bit." She closed her eyes and rested her head on the plane, listening while Cal made his call.

"Sully, it's Cal. There's a situation at the ranch and I need you here, ASAP. No, everyone's fine. Bailey was ambushed, I think. She's fine. The guy's...not. Right. Okay. Thanks." He ended the call and began another. "Jinx, bring me some juice and a snack to the plane. No, it's not for me, you cursed old coot. Bailey's feeling a bit puny. Thanks."

He disconnected that call, set his phone on the ground, and slid his arm around Bailey. She rested her head on him.

"He's a big guy," he whispered.

"Yes."

"He could have…" he cut off his own words, swallowing hard.

"But he didn't," she said. When she first joined the marines, she'd been so full of herself, so certain of her abilities. She'd had the Hollywood notion she could take anyone, that she could beat a man with her bare fists. It had only taken a few wallops from her instructors to quash that notion. The laws of nature always had their way. She could not physically overpower most men. Men were bigger; men were stronger. It was a cruel fact of life for someone who viewed herself as their physical equal. So Bailey had learned to fight harder and, as she'd told Cal that first day, dirtier. She did whatever she needed to do to protect herself and those around her. Weapons were a great equalizer. A man and a woman, each armed with a gun, were an identical playing field. But fighting hand to hand as she'd done today took every ounce of her energy, leaving her weak, empty, and depleted until she refueled.

When Jinx arrived a bit later with the snack, she realized she'd fallen asleep. "How you doing, sweet baby?" Cal whispered.

"I'm fine," she assured him, sitting up away from him. "Also, it's kind of funny you called me sweet, considering."

"You're sweet to me," he said. "Except that first day when you sent a few thousand volts through me."

"I regret nothing," she said.

"Me neither."

Jinx slid off his horse, eyeing them with concern. "What's up? You doing all right, Bailey?"

"Take a peek inside the plane," Cal said, something like pride eking into his tone.

Jinx opened the door and made the same sort of exclamation Cal had. "Where'd that come from?"

"It's an early Christmas present," Bailey said, feeling perkier after the nap and juice. "Surprise."

"That wasn't on my list," Jinx said. "He's waking up. Hello, sunshine."

The man moved around, making noise, cursing loudly and moaning. Cal stood up and hauled the man out of the plane, holding him by the scruff of the neck like a rambunctious puppy. The man was big; Cal was bigger.

"Who sent you?" Cal asked.

In reply, the man spit at him. Or at least he tried to. His lip was too bruised and swollen to do much more than a pathetic sort of whistle that made Cal laugh. "Can you stand?" he asked, letting go of the man who wobbled slightly before attaining his balance. "Excellent," Cal said and then punched him full fisted in the face so the man dropped to the ground, unconscious again.

Bailey watched from her position on the ground with something like envy. She could punch, but not like that. What she wouldn't give to be able to drop a man with one fist to the face.

Sully arrived a few minutes later, by plane this time. Bailey was able to stand by the time he disembarked, along with his pilot.

"You did this?" he asked Bailey, tapping the man on the ground with the toe of his boot.

"It was nothing," Bailey replied, tossing a wink to Jinx and Cal, who knew better.

"Huh. I recognize that mug. I've arrested him twice before, once for assault, once for possession. Both times I handed him over to ICE. They dropped him off over the border, and he hopped back in again. Man." He kicked the dirt, huffing his frustration.

Bailey was a newcomer, but she shared their frustration. There seemed to be no solution to the endless cycle of crime. And the government seemed unwilling or unable to help, maybe both things.

Sully gave Bailey a statement to fill out while he and his pilot loaded the man into their plane. They would take him to the hospital before jail, to have his nose, fingers, and arm set.

By the time everything was over, it was time for supper. "I'm sorry you lost a whole day to this," Bailey said as she and Cal walked side by side to the house.

"That's the least of my worries. We took one of theirs. They're going to try and take one of ours," he said.

"Maybe."

"You don't think?" he asked, his tone hopeful.

"I don't know, Cal. In traditional rules of war, they would realize and recognize the threat. They would understand we won't back down and might begin to cut their losses and move on. It's not worth it to them, really. Eventually it's going to cut into their business, their profit. But there are other factors involved skewing the results."

"What other factors?" he asked.

"Machismo, for one. The fact I'm a woman has to be killing them."

"It's killing me," he joked, putting her head in a headlock and kissing her temple before letting her go.

"There's also Isabel," Bailey said.

He sucked a breath like she'd socked him. "What does Isabel have to do with this?" They reached the porch and faced each other.

"Sully told me what she's been up to." Cal shook his head, trying to protest, unwilling to listen. Bailey rested her hand on his arm. "You need to hear it. Isabel has taken up with the head of the cartel."

"She wouldn't," he protested.

Bailey didn't argue. Nothing she could say would help him believe, especially since he already knew the truth, however much he might want to deny it. She grasped his biceps, catching and holding his eyes. "I've been varying my patrols, mixing it up, keeping it unpredictable. But he was waiting for me. Someone told him I was coming. He wore a helmet and Kevlar. Someone let him know I'd be armed, that I'm a lethal shot."

"How would Isabel know any of that?" he asked.

"She wouldn't."

"What are you saying?" he asked.

"I'm saying I think someone on the ranch is working both sides."

CHAPTER 14

That night was tense and silent. Bailey had a headache from being bashed in the face. Cal wasn't quite angry, but neither did he believe her suggestion someone on the ranch was a traitor.

"Everyone who is with me has been with me for years. We're family. There are no drifters on the crew," he said.

"Whoever it is is likely on drugs, and drugs change a person. Take Isabel, for example."

At that point he actually put his hands over his ears and shook his head like an obstinate child. "I'll stop," she promised, too tired and sore to continue to argue anyway. "But not before I say one more thing: Not believing something doesn't make it not true. And that goes for everything."

"What's that supposed to mean?" he asked.

"You know," she said, eyeing his ring.

He crossed his arms, tucking his ring under his armpit.

"Stubborn," she accused.

"A common trait in these parts," he said.

After that she grabbed an ice pack and went to bed.

The next morning they worked calves, and it was all hands on deck, too busy and exhausting to wonder over the events of the day before. It was Bailey's first such experience, and also the first time she saw Cal physically work the ranch. Most of his day was spent with the business of running the place. But today, wearing a t-shirt, jeans, boots, and a Stetson, he was indiscernible from any other cowboy, except for the fact that he towered above everyone else by a few inches.

The calves had to be separated from their mothers, rounded up, caught, branded, inoculated, and sorted. It was physically exhausting labor on any day, but the thermometer hovered north of ninety, making the work seem harder. Estralita was on hand, along with a couple of hired ladies from town, to dole drinks to the men, an unending job since they became dehydrated so quickly. Bailey stood on a fence and watched. From a distance, they looked like a hive of worker bees, all seeming to know what to do without being told. For someone who enjoyed order and hard work as much as she did, it was a beautiful sight.

"Want to take a turn, little bit?" Cal offered, coming to lean on the fence beside her. She hadn't spoken to him all morning, and she wasn't sure if he was avoiding her or merely busy. Was he the type to hold a grudge? Apparently not if the friendly way he looked at her was any indication.

"You mean brand a calf?" she asked with no small amount of trepidation.

"You can beat a man half senseless, but you draw the line at hurting a cow?"

He grinned and, have mercy, the picture he made was alluring— dusty, dirty, sweat-stained, the hard muscles of his chest straining at his t-shirt. The only white parts of him now were his teeth and hat, which despite the hard day's labor remained remarkably untouched. She had never wanted anything before like she wanted him, and he'd placed himself completely off limits. Bailey was used to going after what she wanted, regardless of the obstacles. But the obstacles in this instance were his principles, his very integrity, something she wouldn't touch because she respected him. It was a vicious circle of honor and desire he'd sucked her into, and it was driving her crazy.

"If men were as cute and innocent as cows, I'd have a harder time beating them. Does it hurt them, really?"

If he noticed the way she looked at him, he pretended not to. "Their hides are pretty thick, much like my head." He reached out to flick her ponytail. "And we use freeze branding now. It's less painful."

"All right." She hopped off the fence and followed him into the pen. They used chutes to hold the frightened calves and tip them on their sides, but Cal wanted to show her the old-fashioned way. He caught a calf and held it while she pressed the frozen brand into its hide, exactly where he showed her. The calf bellowed and fought, but it seemed more fearful than pained. Continuing to follow his instructions, she gave it the inoculation and tagged its ear before he let it go. The calf jumped up, bucked, and would have double kicked her if Cal hadn't picked her up, moving her out of harm's way.

"You're quick," she noted. If her voice sounded shaky, it was from his touch and not the near miss with the cow. She hoped he wouldn't know the difference, but of course he did.

"You're cute," he returned, giving her a slow smile as he set her down.

"What's it worth to you?" she asked.

"More than you know. Ready for another?"

"How many are there?" she asked, tearing her gaze from him so it could rest on the pen full of calves.

"Four thousand," he said and laughed when she did a comic double take. "We break it up, doing about five hundred a day. This is round one. We'll continue until it's finished, taking a break for Sunday." He paused. "So, I think you should stay, at least through calving. Then things will calm down, and we can assess where we are. In terms of security, I mean. But the next few days," he gestured helplessly to the pen behind him. "This is my life, from before sun up until after sundown."

He was a married man. Regardless of whether it was in name only, he was still married. She should go, should flee, should run home and forget she'd ever met him. "What can I do to help?"

"Your normal job. With all of us centered here the next few days, there's going to be lots of room for mischief on the rest of the ranch," he said.

"All right," she heard herself agree. *Weak, Bailey, you're so weak.* He flashed her another smile again and, though they were standing in the center of the hub of activity in full view of the entire ranch staff, it took everything within her not to reach for him, not to stand on her toes, pull him close, and kiss him hard. He was so…capable, so strong, so good and deep. He was everything a man should be. And, like it or not, she was in love with him.

She didn't know what his thoughts were as he stood a foot away from her, hands clenched at his sides, but she figured they were along the same lines. She took a step back and then another. "Think I'll do a quick patrol. Let me know if there's something you think of I can do here. Otherwise, I'm probably in your way."

"Not in my way, never that," he said softly. He swallowed hard and took a breath. "Check in when you're done with your patrol. You're really on your own out there until this is done."

She nodded once and made herself turn and walk away from him. When she was in the air, everything seemed so clear. She needed to go. Staying put was like prolonging torture. Cal wasn't in the right frame of heart or mind for them to work. Why had she said she'd stay? She couldn't; she wouldn't. When she landed, she would tell him and then she would stick to her original timeline and leave in a few days.

But when she landed and went to find him, he was still in the midst of hard, manual labor. She stood on the fencepost and watched again, admiring him while he worked. The muscles and sinews in his arms and back were impressive, but more than that she enjoyed his work style. He was a man other men looked to, and that meant something to her. She had grown up with a strong father, a leader of men. She wouldn't be able to accept anything less in someone she desired. Cal was that kind of person, the sort who made those around him want to work harder, be better, give more of themselves.

He caught sight of her on the fence and tipped his hat to her, tossing her a smile. *Maybe I could stay a few days more,* she found herself thinking as her eyes followed him. Then she turned away with a groan of frustration. "So weak, Bailey." At the very least she could make herself useful. After a word with Estralita, she grabbed the keys to a truck and drove herself to town.

CHAPTER 15

The next day Bailey worked in the kitchen. Her morning patrol was complete. The ranch was quiet, minus the activity now taking place at its center. She could neither stomach another day of boredom nor a day of staring at Cal, mooney-eyed, as he worked. So she asked Estralita if she could make supper. Estralita's reaction had been a bit more insecure than Bailey would have imagined, as if she thought maybe Bailey was trying to take over her kitchen. Bailey put her mind at ease by asking if she would handle dessert.

"I can cook okay, but I'm hopeless at baking," she confessed to the older woman.

"I can make peach cobbler, it's the *Señor's* favorite."

Bailey hugged her. "Estralita, you are worth your weight in gold."

"I'll show you how sometime, yes?" Estralita replied, returning her hug.

"You can try, but I'm kind of hopeless when it comes to anything that involves flour," Bailey told her.

But now, in the kitchen and working on supper, she felt soothed and at peace. Cooking always had that effect, regardless of how little she did it. She was often too busy to bother but, as with everything she did, she gave it a thousand percent. She hadn't stopped trying until she'd perfected the recipe she was making tonight. It was her showstopper. As it was likely the only meal she would ever cook here, it had to be amazing.

She made the rice, assembled everything, and left it to stew before heading outside. Sully arrived as she reached her spot at the fence.

"Hey, you made it," Bailey said, bumping his shoulder as he came to stand beside her.

"Wouldn't have missed it, thanks for the invite. How's it going here?" he nodded toward the hive of men now putting the calves through their paces with a practiced ferocity.

"I don't know. I've been in the kitchen all day. The rest of the ranch has been quiet, disturbingly so. Wouldn't you think it would be the other way? They know calving is going on. This is their chance to create havoc. But it's crickets out there. It's making me antsy."

"Either you scared them off or they're taking their time, planning something big," Sully said. "Guess what I heard at the jail the other day?"

"What's that?" she asked. She linked her arm with his. Somewhere along the way her mild loathing of him had turned to a brotherly sort of affection, and he seemed to feel the same about her.

"They have a nickname for you."

"The jail?"

"The members of the cartel who are currently incarcerated," he said.

"What is it?" she asked, already smiling in amused anticipation.

"*La diabla loca.* Crazy she devil."

"They may be terrible people, but that's a cool nickname," she said.

"That's a cool nickname," he agreed.

Cal caught sight of them and jogged over, resting his hands on the fence on either side of Bailey's. "Anything to report, Major Dunbar?"

"All's right as rain, boss," she said.

"With an expression like that, you're sounding almost local," he said. "Hey, Sul," he turned to the ranger, smiling. "What brings you out? Some kind of trouble?"

"No, some kind of supper. *La diabla loca* is cooking."

Cal bestowed his attention once again on Bailey. "Is that right?"

"How'd you know he was talking about me?"

"Who else, darlin'? Paella?"

"Yes, sir."

"Well, I can hardly wait. Want to come in here a bit?" he offered.

She held up her hands, palms out. "Don't want to get my fingers dirty today."

"Sissy," he said. He took off his hat and placed it on her head before turning to rejoin the fray.

"You know, 'round here giving a woman your hat is as good as a proposal," Sully said.

"I think I'm about ten years too late on his proposal," Bailey said, somewhat sadly.

"Let me tell you something about Cal. He's tenacious. That's what made him a good quarterback. That's what makes him a good rancher. He also despises change. At some point he's got to realize he has to let go of Isabel and accept there are some things that have to move along, despite how much he tries to hold on."

"In the meantime, every day that goes by makes me look a little more foolish," she said.

"No one who knows you could ever think you're a fool," Sully said.

"Thanks," she said. "I should go back inside, check on things."

"Want some help?" he asked.

"It won't bother you to be in the kitchen doing women's work while the men are out here?" she asked.

"Honey, I've worked calves before. Believe me when I tell you the kitchen is a far, far better place to be."

An hour later, he was ready to change his mind. "Has anyone ever told you you're terrifying?"

"Mostly my little sisters," Bailey replied unconcernedly. They had arranged tables outside, making one giant line, along with chairs and hay bales enough for everybody to have a seat. Taking Cal's directive to "make herself at home" seriously, she snooped until she located tablecloths and place settings enough for everyone. Then she sent Sully up a ladder to hang string lights she found. There was only one oak tree beside the house, but it was massive enough to provide all the shade they'd need. Lastly, she found some clean Mason jars and cut flowers for bouquets.

The men limped over, dirty, exhausted, famished. But when they saw the long table decorated and loaded with food, they perked up. Soon it became a party atmosphere with laughing and talking and eating, lots and lots of eating.

When the food was finished, Jinx's sons, Corrie and Jonah, brought out their guitars and began to play softly. The sun sank low, and the oppressive heat began to wane. Cal slid his arm behind Bailey's chair and leaned close to talk to her.

"Are you happy?" he whispered.

"Exponentially so. You?"

"For the first time in a long, long time, yes I am. Thank you for supper tonight."

"It was the least I could do while you all are working so hard."

"It really wasn't," he said, his eyes sliding to the middle distance, probably to his past and memories.

"What did Isabel do during calving season?" she asked.

"In the early days, when we still actually liked each other, she used to come out and watch, talk, socialize. The last few years we were together she went away, had a girls weekend or went presumably by herself. In retrospect I'm not certain she was actually alone during those times."

"I'm sorry, Cal. Really, really sorry for the way things turned out, for the pain your uncoupling has caused you. It's unfair, and it stinks, and every bad thing."

"The upside is I think the shock and denial of it all are starting to wear off. The downside is that the grief and pain are setting in." He sighed and his fingers skimmed lightly along her back. "Sweet girl, I think this old dog is kind of a mess."

"You don't get to corner the market on mess, sir. We're each a mess, in our own special way."

"What's your mess, Bailey? Because from where I sit, I only see the good."

"I'm a workaholic control freak daredevil perfectionist who is too often out of touch with my emotions."

"But what's your mess? Because all that sounds pretty good to me," he said.

She reached out and smoothed the flyaway hair at his temple. His hair was a bit of a mess, twisted and bent from a long, sweaty day beneath his Stetson. He leaned into her touch, smiling. "I bought a ticket for home."

He froze. "When?"

"Friday, six days."

He swallowed hard. "Why?"

"Because we can't keep fooling ourselves with this, pretending we can go on like this with no consequences. Either you're going to break and hate yourself or you're not going to break and I'll eventually resent you. We're friends, we're pals, in the kindest and purest sense of the words. I want to keep it like that, to go out on a good note while we're both heart whole with no regrets."

"He clasped her hand and held it between both of his. "I want to…I want, Bailey. I want so much."

"I know you do, but not enough to do something about it," she said.

He gave her hand a squeeze and let it go. "I understand. If this is what you feel is best, then I'll support you."

She smiled and nodded, but inwardly she was disappointed. She hadn't meant the ticket as an ultimatum but there was a secret little part of her that hoped he would take it so.

"What time is your flight on Friday? I'll make sure I'm available to drive you to the airport."

"Sully has business in San Antonio that day. He's offered to take me," she said. She couldn't do the airport goodbye with Cal; she just couldn't. It would be hard enough to do it here, away from prying eyes.

"Oh, okay," he said. They settled into awkward silence. Bailey stood.

"I should get this cleaned up."

"I'll help," he said.

"Don't be crazy. You've worked all day. Relax, please. I've got this." She squeezed his shoulder briefly and began gathering dishes and silverware. Music and conversation buzzed around her, and she wasn't sure if they helped to fill up her empty pieces or make her more aware of them. Either way, she was glad for something to do, for any task that kept her from thinking or feeling too much.

CHAPTER 16

On Sunday it stormed. It was the first rain Bailey had witnessed in Texas, and she was unprepared for the powerful way it would descend on the ranch, darkening the sky with billowing, heaving black clouds, drenching the soil with a torrential downpour, thundering through the buildings, illuminating the sky with violent slashes of lightning. For a long time she stood at the window, caught up in the beauty and passion of it.

"I love a good storm," Cal said, coming to stand alongside her. "My favorite part is after, when it's still cool, before the humidity realizes how long it's been absent and rushes to make a return appearance. It always feels a bit like a clean slate, like starting over."

"It's beautiful," she said in an awed whisper. She would never be able to tell him how very much she had come to love the ranch, how hard it would be for her to leave for a number of reasons, only one of which was him. Her childhood had been filled with multiple moves, thanks to her military father. Her adulthood had been much the same, due to her own service. The closest she had ever come to feeling at home was in Africa. And now here.

Her skin prickled with the heat of his nearness behind her. She wanted nothing more than to lean into him, to feel his powerful arms slide around her, to tip her face to his for a kiss. It was becoming exponentially harder to rein in her wild desires. She was like a constant exposed nerve, except instead of feeling pain she felt *want, want, want.* She ached with the need to touch him, to feel his skin beneath her fingers. She inhaled, smelling the clean, male scent of him. So close, but so far.

"Bailey," he whispered. His hand reached out to touch her bicep and she shivered from the innocuous little contact. She sensed his arms reaching for her, but before she could pivot into them, the front door opened and closed.

Bailey remained staring out the window, and it was Cal who pivoted away from her, facing the newcomer. "Isabel."

"I need to talk to you," Isabel announced in her customarily imperious tone.

"Okay," Cal drawled.

"Alone," Isabel clarified.

"No," Bailey said, finally tearing her gaze away from the window to face the other woman. "After what you threatened last time, I'm not leaving you alone with him."

"He's my husband," Isabel said.

"He's my boss, and it's my job to keep him safe," Bailey said.

"Cal," Isabel all but whined, turning pleading eyes in his direction.

"Bailey stays," he said quietly.

Isabel gave a wounded little sound but quickly recovered. "Fine. Let her hear what I have to say. I need more money."

That proclamation was greeted with stunned silence. Eventually Cal found his voice. "How is that possible? I gave you ten thousand dollars not two weeks ago."

She shrugged. "Living is expensive."

"Are you on drugs?" he blurted.

"Cal, come on," she said, aiming for a laugh and failing mightily.

"Don't lie to me, Isabel. Are you on drugs?"

"I take a little something as a pick me up now and then. It's no big deal. You know I did coke a few times when I was in college, and I never got hooked. It's like that."

"Is that where all my money is going?"

"It's my money, too," she yelled. She took a breath and forced calm back into her voice. "Hey, come on, it's not like I'm asking for that much. Five thousand would be great, and I promise not to come back again for at least a month."

"No," he said, shaking his head.

She scowled, but before she could respond, he continued.

"Is it true you're dating the head of the cartel?"

"Dating's a strong word for what we do," she said with a saucy little grin. Bailey could almost feel the pain knife through Cal. She wanted to hit the woman, to physically toss her from the house. But so far she hadn't done anything but have a tantrum and there was no need for Bailey to interfere into their business.

"You must have lost fifteen pounds in the last month," Cal said. "I don't know why I didn't see it before."

"That's the best part. It's like I don't even have to try to keep the weight off anymore. Best diet ever," she said, her flippant tone in sharp contrast to the anxious set of her features. "Cal, I really need that money."

"Why?"

"It's not for drugs, I swear. It's for food and gas and, um, clothes and makeup and stuff."

"Isabel, you have no mortgage, no rent, no car payment, and I set up an account for you to cover all your utilities, gas, and food. You've blown through ten thousand dollars in thirteen days, and I'd venture most of it has gone into your veins or up your nose. You don't need more money. You need help."

"Don't tell me what I need. You don't know. You've never known." She put her hands to her temples, rubbing them in frustration. "I don't know why I thought I could come here and you would help. You hate me. You've always hated me."

"You know that's not true," he said.

"Then just give me the money. What's the big deal? You've got enough of it."

He shook his head. "I won't give you money, but I'll pay for you to go to an inpatient drug treatment center, somewhere good, somewhere far away like Malibu or Arizona."

"Those places are for broken down celebrities and junkies," she said. "Maybe that's what you want, Cal. Are you going to get a photographer to follow me and publish a picture? 'Former Miss America Checks Into Rehab.' Or maybe, 'Former NFL Quarterback's Wife's Brush With Addiction.' Which do you think will play better for the folks at home?"

"It's not about that, Isabel. And it's not for public consumption. We can find a clinic that specializes in privacy. I'll call my old agent, he'll know." He withdrew his phone, and she stamped her foot.

"I'm not going to rehab. Are you even hearing me? I don't have a problem. I am not addicted to drugs. Stop trying to make this seem like something it's not. I need some money, that's all. And you owe me that much, Cal. We're still married. Or have you forgotten?" Her eyes landed accusingly on Bailey.

"I haven't forgotten. That's why I'm making the offer. It's rehab or nothing."

She pushed him, or tried to. Both hands landed on his chest and gave a hard shove, but he was taller and stronger and the gesture was ineffectual. Bailey tensed but otherwise didn't intervene.

Cal lightly grasped Isabel's wrists. "Stop it," he said gently and the gentleness seemed to be her undoing. She was spoiling for a fight, wanted to face his anger and wrath, but had no idea what to do with kindness and, worst of all, pity.

"Let go of me," she screeched, bucking like a wild thing to get away from his grasp. He opened his grip and let her go. One of her palms reared back, ready to strike him hard across the cheek, and this time Bailey intervened because he was going to let it happen, going to let her hit him as much as she wanted, as hard as she wanted until she was spent. But Bailey couldn't take it, couldn't stand to see him hurt one minute longer. So she caught Isabel's wrist and twisted her arm behind her back, pinning her to the wall in one smooth motion.

"I don't think you really want to pick on someone your own size," Bailey said.

"Let go of me," Isabel screamed, followed by an ugly wave of invectives, both in English and in Spanish. Bailey kept her pinned until she wore herself out and stopped struggling.

"Are you done?" she asked when the angry energy faded out of Isabel, leaving her drained and exhausted.

Isabel nodded. Bailey let her go and took a step back, keeping a defensive pose in case the calm demeanor was a fraud.

"I hate you," Isabel said, her eyes settling first on Cal and then on Bailey. "I hope you both die."

Cal remained silent, but his breathing was labored, pained. "I don't hate you," Bailey said and meant it. "I'm incredibly sorry for you." The woman had had perfection and tossed it away, both in her marriage and in her personal life. Someone like that could only be worthy of the deepest sort of pity.

"Don't be," Isabel said, her eyes filling with angry tears. "I'm happy, *finally* happy," she added with another vicious look at Cal. "My life is perfect, and I wouldn't change a thing."

"Well then it seems your business here is done," Bailey said.

"Are you going to let her throw me out of my own house?" Isabel demanded.

"You need to go," Cal agreed.

Somewhere in there her anger was refueled enough to allow her to take another shot at Bailey. She drew back a fist and swung, but Bailey was ready for her and ducked easily aside. The momentum sent Isabel stumbling almost drunkenly forward a few steps. She grasped a chair to keep from falling over. It would have been funny if it weren't so tragically sad. Here was a woman whose life was unraveling before their eyes, who refused help, who had no idea how much danger she was really in.

When she regained her balance, she brushed her hands down her well-tailored shirt, dusting at pretend dirt, and then, head up, walked out the door. A minute later they heard her car roar to life and drive away.

"Excuse me," Cal said. Turning, he made his way out of the room.

He kept his back to her, but Bailey could still see him wiping his eyes before he rounded the corner into his bedroom.

She resumed her post by the window, but the storm outside had lost its appeal. What before had seemed like a promise of renewal now seemed ominous. She shivered and ran her hands up and down her arms, taken with a sudden chill.

CHAPTER 17

Alone in his room, Cal pulled out his phone and called his brother.

"Hey, aren't you in the middle of branding?" Cam answered.

"I thought you'd be nostalgic for it, so I'm calling to commiserate," Cal answered, scrubbing at his eyes a final time.

"You know I had a dream once I was putting a calf in a shoot. Woke up trying to truss Maggie with the bed sheet. Freaked us both out pretty bad," Cam said, giving Cal a much needed laugh. "How's it going with Bailey?"

"Good, it's really good. She's implemented a lot of positive security changes, and she's become a friend. A good friend."

"How's that going over with Is?"

"About as well as you'd expect," Cal said.

Cam laughed. "I'd say Is would scratch her eyes out, but something tells me Bailey can probably hold her own."

"That she can," Cal agreed. He took a breath. *Say it, just tell him. Get it over with and the truth will be out there and you can move on.*

"Hey, speaking of Is, I wanted to talk to you about something," Cam said.

Cal gripped the phone tighter. "Yeah? What's that?"

"I have some vacation time coming up and Maggie's making me use it this time. We were thinking of getting a house on the gulf, and we want you and Is to come."

"You...you do?"

"Absolutely. Maggie is, er, extremely family centric. She's really been on me about the lack on our end, and she's right. We don't see you guys enough. Someday we'll have kids, and we want them to know their uncle and aunt. I want them to see the ranch, to know how we grew up."

"Okay. I'll get back to you. Kind of crazy busy right now, you know."

"Sure, absolutely. I remember those days. But, Cal, I meant what I said. I want us to spend more time together. It's ridiculous how rarely we see each other."

"Agreed," Cal said, his throat beginning to close again.

"Give the calves a kiss for me."

"Do the same to Maggie," Cal said, clearing his throat.

"I will, but if I try to brand her again, she's going to be pretty mad," Cam said and Cal laughed again. They disconnected and Cal sat on his bed a long time, staring at nothing.

The next morning was Monday, the last day of branding. Bailey started with the men before dawn and worked the entire day. When the sun fully rose, Cal disappeared into the house for a few minutes and handed her a Stetson.

"This was my first hat when I was fourteen." He placed it on her head, ceremonially, she thought, and then handed her a pair of sturdy leather gloves. "To keep those fingers clean," he added with a smile.

"Too late for that," she said, holding her dirt-crusted fingers aloft for his inspection.

"I like a girl with a bit of muck on her," he said, flicking her hat before he disappeared again.

That night they sat on the porch in the glider, too tired to talk or even move.

"Going to have to cut my boots off," Bailey said. She was accustomed to hard, physical labor, but nothing had prepared her for a full day of ranch work. Bailey felt like everything hurt and maybe she was dying, but she wouldn't say so because if he could do it and keep functioning, then so could she.

Cal picked up her legs, unlaced her boots, and rested her feet in his lap.

"Those can't smell good," she noted.

"I like a girl who smells like a hard day's work," he mused.

"You have odd tastes in women, sir," she returned, and it was the last thing she remembered until she woke up in her bed the next morning, fully clothed.

Cal acted like nothing was amiss, so Bailey followed his lead. They ate breakfast together like usual, drank their coffee in companionable silence, and then she couldn't take it anymore.

"Did you carry me to bed last night?"

"This is Texas. It's state law that whenever you happen upon a sleeping female, you carry her somewhere," he said.

"That must explain your high rate of sleep kidnappings," she said. "And thank you."

He tipped his coffee to her. "I'd like to do your patrol with you this morning. On horseback, if it's all the same to you."

"Sure," she agreed. "Why, though?"

"Can't a man see his own ranch without having a reason?"

"Yes, but not you. You have a reason for everything."

"You're leaving in a few days, and I want to soak up some time with you while you're still here," he said.

"Oh."

"Plus yesterday was rough and nothing clears out the cobwebs like a good, long ride," he added.

"True," she agreed.

"And I thought it might increase my street cred to be seen with *la diabla loca*."

"That's enough reasons," she said.

"You sure? Because I could keep going."

"I'm certain, sir," she replied.

They saddled their horses, packed up their rifles, and set off. Bailey felt antsy and expectant, and she wondered if Cal felt the same. The last few days had been quiet, too quiet. Now that the ranch was returning to normal, she half expected something big to happen, some sort of retaliation or action on the south pasture. She wondered if Cal felt the same and if it was why he had asked to go with her.

She felt his eyes on her often through the day, but when she turned to face him, he appeared not to be looking at her. And then she got caught up staring at him and had to turn away when he turned to look. It was like being fifteen all over again, only when she was fifteen she'd had no interest in boys and certainly never a crush of this magnitude. Bailey had been a late bloomer in every sense of the word, drawing out her tomboy childhood for as long as humanly possible, much to her father's delight. It had about killed him when she went on her first date at the Naval academy, especially because it had been with the creeper who wouldn't take no for an answer.

They rode for a long time, much longer than was probably necessary for a patrol. But the time together was peaceful, restorative. They didn't talk much beyond pointing something out to the other, but that was the way they both preferred it. Beyond words—a mutual understanding of shared interests and friendship.

When they arrived back at the house, they spied a large cardboard box sitting in the middle of the front walkway. It grabbed their attention, diverting them from the barn.

"Did you order another dress?" Cal asked.

"Not hardly," Bailey replied.

"I didn't order anything. Maybe Estralita dropped off a stew. I can't imagine why she'd leave it outside, but it looks like it's leaking." He slid down off his horse and headed for the package.

Bailey tipped her head at the box, staring at the liquid oozing from inside. Then she vaulted off her horse, threw herself at an unsuspecting Cal, and tackled him to the ground.

He landed on his back with a thud, Bailey on top of him. "Are you doing a repeat of your first day? Why'd you take me down, little bit?" he asked, his hand caressing her hair.

She shook her head, unable to formulate the necessary words.

His eyes narrowed in concern. "Honey, what's wrong?"

"Don't look in that box," she finally said.

He froze and turned his head to look at the box. Realization began to dawn on him, and he struggled to get up, to return to the box. Bailey tried to hold him down.

"Cal, look at me. Don't. Don't look in that box. We'll call Sully. Please, please, please…" He was too strong for her. She fought him, but he shook her easily aside and, with a shaking hand, peeled open the top of the box and peered inside. And then he screamed, a primal, horrible scream ripped from somewhere deep. Bailey put her hands over her ears, blocking the sound, but it was too late. She could never unhear it, just as he could never unsee what he had seen in the box.

He stumbled a few feet away to a rose bush and heaved a few times, then stumbled a few more steps and sank to his knees. Bailey sprang up, knelt beside him, and tried to gather him to her, but in his shock he pushed her away and tried to get back to the box.

"No," she said, shaking him by his shoulders. When that failed to work, she slapped him across the face, hard. He jumped and stared at her. "Do not look at it again," she commanded, her fingers digging into his shoulders.

He nodded dumbly and sat staring blankly at the horizon. Meanwhile Bailey reached for his phone and dialed Sully.

"I need you immediately. Take the plane." She hung up without explanation and called Jinx.

"I need you at the house. Now."

She could hear Jinx's boots scrambling on gravel as he sprinted from the barn, no easy task for a man of his age, but he made it in record time.

"What is it? What's wrong?" he asked, taking in the scene before him, Cal sitting on the ground like a zombie, Bailey attempting to hold him like a child, a large box blocking the path. Like a beacon, the box drew him, but Bailey stood.

"No," she yelled with so much force he stopped short. "Come here. Do not look in the box."

He gave the box a wide berth, sidestepping it as he made his way to them. He knelt beside Cal. He had known him since birth and never seen him this way. He rested his hand on the boy's shoulder. "What's wrong with him? Is he snakebit?"

"He's had a bad shock." Her glance fell to the box and quickly away. "Help me get him inside."

They levered Cal to his feet, no easy task as he was much taller than both of them. With effort, they half carried him down the hall to his room and laid him in his bed. He seemed to rally slightly and clutched at Bailey's hands as if terrified she was going to leave.

"I'm right here," she soothed. "You're all right, Jinx and I are here. We won't leave you." She sat by him in the large bed, smoothing her hand over his sweaty hair. His face was clammy, colorless. She wondered if he would need medical attention for his shock, but Sully would help her decide when he arrived.

"Bailey what's in the box?" Jinx whispered.

Bailey didn't want to say, didn't want to risk setting Cal off again. A pad of paper and pen rested beside the bed. She reached for it and wrote one word.

Isabel.

"Oh, mercy," Jinx said. His knees buckled and he groped for the wall behind him. She watched him to make sure he wouldn't faint or have a heart attack. With effort, he took a few deep breaths and seemed to pull himself together, at least a bit. "I should go keep watch until Sully arrives," he said at last, quietly.

She nodded and returned her attention to Cal, still gently smoothing her hand over his head. She peered closer at his pupils. They were large and he was still somewhere far away, not yet able to return to himself and be present.

Sully's plane arrived a little while later. She heard his loud exclamation from the lawn, and then he was beside them, almost as shaken and pale as Cal had been.

"How's…?" he began, but his voice broke and he couldn't get any further.

"I kind of wonder if he needs to go to the ER." She turned her attention back to Cal. He wouldn't want to, she knew. He would hate to be in public now, to have everyone looking at him, talking about him, pitying him. Tears came to her eyes. She mashed her face to her elbow, pushing them back and *that* was what finally brought Cal around.

"Bailey," he croaked, his hand smoothing along hers.

She sniffled and pressed her palm to his cheek. "Do you want to go to the hospital?"

He shook his head almost violently.

"Will you take a sedative?" she asked.

He nodded.

"Jinx," she called because she could hear him in the living room.

"I heard," he replied. His mother had been sick for a while and had every conceivable medicine at her disposal. It was illegal and possibly unethical to use her medicine for everyone and everything else, but that was essentially what happened after she passed. Her personal pharmacy had turned into a dispensary for anything and everything on the ranch.

Jinx returned a while later with a pill and a glass of water. Cal downed it. A few minutes later he fell gratefully asleep, pulled into blissful unconsciousness by the weight of the pill.

At last Bailey felt like she could leave him. She, Sully, and Jinx stepped back onto the lawn, keeping their distance from the box.

"What exactly is in the box?" Bailey asked. She had no desire to look, not now, not ever.

"Her head and hands," Sully rasped. "If you didn't look, how did you know?"

"The fluid leaking from the box. I've seen death before." She hadn't known who was in the box, of course, but she'd suspected. And the sound Cal made confirmed it. She closed her eyes, trying to push back the sound and the vision of Cal's pain. She hoped never to see another human in that much pain again for as long as she lived.

Sully reached for her hand and gave it a squeeze. At first Bailey resisted the urge to be comforted, and then she realized Sully might be seeking his own comfort. He had known Isabel a long time, had likely socialized with her, dined with her, maybe even danced with her. And now she was gone in the worst possible way. So she hugged him, and he hugged her fiercely in return, burying his face in her hair and letting a few tears fall.

"I've never...that was...how am I gonna...?" They hugged for a while until eventually both of them pulled themselves together and let go. "All right. I called the crime lab. They'll be here soon. We'll do statements and all that goes with it then. For now let's sit and keep vigil." They sat on the steps, looking anywhere but at the box. After a while trucks began to roll up the long lane. Sully breathed a sigh of relief. Bailey didn't know if it was because reinforcements had arrived or because he could focus on work. While he and Jinx went to talk to the newcomers, she slipped away and went back to Cal, preferring to keep vigil with him. She sat in the chair beside the bed and watched him sleep until Sully arrived with a statement for her to fill out.

She did so, downed a bowl of cold stew, forced down a glass of water, and returned to Cal's side. The men went away. Sully came to say goodbye. "Call if you need anything," he whispered. "I'll let you know what we find out."

She nodded. "Thanks, Sully. Try to get some rest."

"You, too. Keep me updated on Cal."

"Will do."

Jinx arrived next, keeping watch with her. He looked all his years then, old and tired. "I've never seen anything like this," he whispered after a while.

"There's nothing that can prepare you for a day like today, but you did well, Jinx. No one could have done better."

"I didn't like her, but..." he trailed off.

"I know, me too."

He sighed and the sound was exhausted. "You can go, Jinx. I'll stay."

"I'd argue, but I think he'd prefer you," Jinx said.

"I don't know about that," Bailey replied.

"I do. Good night, Miss Bailey."

"Good night, sir," she said, standing to give him a hug.

After he left, she sat by the bed again, resuming watch. Cal didn't stir. So deeply did he sleep that she checked him a few times to make sure he was still breathing. Finding that he was, she sat back down and stared, counting the hours, thinking, planning. After a while she rested her head on the bed. At some point she drifted to sleep.

CHAPTER 18

She woke sometime later to Cal petting her head. She sat up, blinking at him in the darkness. Did he find it odd to have her there?

"In Africa, grief isn't solitary. It's shared between friends," she explained. He patted the bed beside him. She climbed over and lay down beside him. The room was dark. She couldn't make out more than his silhouette.

"Can I bring you some food or water?" she offered.

He shook his head. His throat worked, swallowing convulsively with renewed memories.

"Can I hold you?" she whispered.

He nodded. She shifted, drawing his head onto her chest in a motherly gesture of comfort. The dam broke and he sobbed, clutching her close as he drenched her shirt with emotion. She hoped it would be enough, that it would all come spilling out and ease the ache inside him, but of course it wouldn't. It would take time—days and weeks and months and maybe even years to purge all that was in his heart. Bailey didn't speak a word, didn't try to tell him everything would be okay or to let it go. She simply held on and let it happen, let the tears eke out of him little by little until he was spent and fell back asleep.

And even then she didn't let go. She held him until she fell asleep, their bodies clutched together like two halves of a whole.

In the morning when she woke, Cal was gone. She rolled out of bed and went to the kitchen where she saw him sitting at the table, staring at nothing. She made a pot of coffee and, when it was finished, poured him a generous cup and set it before him.

"Thanks," he said on autopilot.

"What can I do?" she asked, pouring her own cup and sitting down across from him.

He shook his head. "I have to call my brother," he choked.

"Would you like me to do it for you?" she asked.

"I should be the one."

"You don't have to. It's going to be hard for him to hear it, no matter who gives him the news."

"No, he'll take it better from his wife." He pulled out his phone and stared at it before handing it to her. "Her name is Maggie. Call her and let her tell him."

"All right. Do you want to hear, or do you want me to go in the other room?"

He nodded toward the other room. Bailey took the phone and stepped away. She found the number for Maggie and pushed the button.

"Hey, ornery," Maggie answered on the first ring, her voice warm and full of sunshine. Despite herself, Bailey smiled. "You up with the cows this morning or something?"

"Uh, hi, this is Bailey Dunbar, I work for Cal."

There was a pause and then, "Is Cal okay? Is there a problem?"

"Cal's fine, but there is a problem." Bailey squeezed her eyes closed. "I'm sorry to tell you that Cal's wife, Isabel, has died."

There was a pause, and then Maggie's voice returned to the line, shakier than before. "What happened?"

"She was murdered, presumably by a local cartel."

"I...I...what?"

"I understand this is extremely shocking. I'm sure Cal will be able to fill in some details for you when he's able. He's, uh, having a difficult time right now. He was hoping you could tell his brother for him. He thought it might be easier coming from you."

"Of course, absolutely. I just...wow. Okay. Sorry, I'm in shock. I'll make flight arrangements. We'll try to be there today."

"I'm sure Cal will appreciate that," Bailey replied.

"I should go tell Cam. Is there anything you need, anything we can bring?" Maggie offered.

"Your husband works for my father, doesn't he?" Bailey asked.

She could almost hear Maggie blinking at the rapid subject change. "Yes. We both love and respect him a great deal."

"I need to talk to him. I know it's a bad time, but if you could have him call me when he's up for it, I'd really appreciate it."

"When he's able, I'll have him give you a call. Thank you for letting us know. I'm sure this hasn't been an easy call for you to make."

"It's fine. I'm just incredibly sorry to be the bearer of such bad news."

"I understand. Goodbye, Bailey. I'll let you know our flight arrangements as soon as they're made."

"I'll make sure to have someone at the airport to meet you," Bailey promised.

"Thank you."

They disconnected and Bailey called Sully. "I know you're crazy busy right now, but I need a favor."

"Name it," he said, and so she did.

Two hours later, she, Jinx, and Sully stood at the entrance to the bunkhouse. The men stood warily before them. Since yesterday the mood had been silent, somber. Today it was worse because no one knew what she was about to say.

"I need to tell you that what's about to happen here is all on me. Cal trusts you completely. He said you're family to him. But that's separate from me and my job here. If anyone feels bad about this, it's on me, not him," she said.

One of them raised a hand. "What's about to happen here?"

Bailey looked at Sully who opened the door. A K9 unit entered with its handler. "Drug sweep," she said. She expected a few protests, but everyone regarded her in silence. Maybe protests would have happened except yesterday pushed everything else out of everyone's minds, even the unfairness of a surprise drug check.

The dog made its way sedately through the building, bed by bed, locker by locker. Bailey began to breathe easier, hoping she was wrong. And then, near the very end, the dog sat and looked at its handler. The silence in the room shifted from somber to stunned.

"Whose bunk is this?" Sully asked. No one answered. "Whose bunk?" he repeated, more forcefully this time.

Jinx stepped forward. "It belongs to Corrie, my son."

All eyes swiveled to Corrie who began hedging away. "There's nothing in there," he said, putting his hands up. Sully took his hands and cuffed them.

"Let's check then," he said.

"You can't," Corrie said. "That stuff's mine."

"It's Cal's property. We need his permission, not yours," Sully said.

"Cal didn't give permission. She just said so," Corrie replied, indicating Bailey with a nod of his head.

"I'm the foreman here. I give permission," Jinx said. "Open it up."

Sully did a quick sweep of the locker and came away with a baggie of what looked like fine brown powder. The dog's handler took it and held it up to the light. "Heroin."

"That's not mine," Corrie said, his tone turning desperate. "Someone planted that there."

"Who?" Jinx barked.

Corrie's head swiveled desperately around the room, finally landing on Bailey. "Her. She did it."

"Why would she do that?" Sully asked.

"Because, uh, she wants to get us in trouble for Isabel's death. She probably killed her. Everyone knows she threatened her."

"You think Bailey killed Isabel, hacked her to pieces, planted her on the front walk for Cal to find, then planted heroin on you?" Jinx asked, his tone disgusted. "Boy, at least have the guts to admit it when you done wrong."

Corrie swallowed convulsively and looked away, fastening his gaze on the far wall. Sully sighed, something he had unconsciously been doing all day, and read Corrie his rights.

The handler and dog departed, along with the heroin. Sully led Corrie outside, followed by Jinx and Bailey.

"Jinx, could you please go to the house and sit with Cal a while? I'd feel so much better if I knew he wasn't alone," Bailey said.

Jinx regarded her with a stare. She held his gaze. At last he nodded once. "How long should I plan to stay there?"

"An hour," Bailey said.

Jinx disappeared. Bailey turned to Sully. "I need to talk to him."

"He's a prisoner in my custody," Sully said. "I can't just give him to you."

"Of course not. But I know you have a lot of paperwork to fill out. Maybe you could use Cal's office for about an hour while I keep watch for you."

Like Jinx, Sully gave her a solitary nod.

"Could you switch his cuffs to the front for me?" she asked. "Make him more comfortable like."

Sully complied, cuffing Corrie's hands in front of his body instead of behind. Then he turned and walked toward Cal's office. "Wait, what's happening? Where are you going?" Corrie called. "Sully, don't leave me alone with her. Come back."

"Come with me," Bailey said. She grasped Corrie's bicep and frog marched him to the tack room, closing and locking the door behind them. She had set up a small table with a couple of chairs, just in case, and now she used them, positioning Corrie in the seat across from hers.

"I want names, locations, details of your contacts," she said.

"I don't have any contacts. I told you I don't know where that stuff came from. I don't even do drugs." He was clearly lying. Now that she was looking, she could see the twitchy eyes of a user. It had probably been a while since his last fix, and he was coming down, needing to refuel. That worked well to her advantage.

"I'm going to ask politely one more time. I want names, locations, and details of your contacts."

"I don't know anything," he insisted.

Bailey reached across the table and snapped his middle finger. He roared with pain, tears springing immediately to his eyes and rolling down his face.

"Now, I can snap that back in for you easily. All the pain will be forgotten. In fact, you'll get such an endorphin rush it will make the high you get from opium seem like child's play. Or you have nine more fingers. What happens next is up to you." She pressed her palms to the table and leaned forward. "I want names, locations, and details of your contacts."

"I only know my supplier's name," he yelled. He held his hand aloft, staring at his oddly bent finger in horror.

Bailey reached across the table and snapped his finger back into place. For a moment she thought he was going to pass out with the relief of it, but then he seemed to settle down and come back to his senses. "Start talking, and if I don't like your answers, you'll feel it."

They talked for an hour, and then she released him back into Sully's hands, weepy and shaking, clutching his fingers possessively to his chest. Almost as soon as she finished with Corrie, her phone rang.

"Hi, Major Dunbar, this is Cameron Ridge, Cal's brother." His voice sounded slightly hoarse with suppressed emotion, but otherwise he seemed able to carry on the sort of conversation they needed to have.

"Lieutenant Ridge, I'm so very sorry about your sister-in-law, sir."

"Thank you. I had no idea the situation was so serious down there. Is Cal in danger?"

"Everyone is in danger until the situation is resolved," she said.

He must have read something in her tone because he paused before he answered. "I take it you have a resolution in mind, Major."

He didn't have an accent at the beginning of the call, but with those last words the twang began to seep in, and he sounded like Cal. "Yes, sir. But I'm going to need a few things."

"I'm listening," he said, and Bailey filled him in on her plan.

CHAPTER 19

Cal and Bailey were on the porch when Cam and Maggie arrived. He had been quiet all day. Bailey had remained near his side, quietly reassuring like a farm dog. As they sat on the glider, sharing their customary glass of iced tea, he gripped her hand, holding it like a lifeline.

The truck pulled up, the same one that had brought Bailey to the ranch a few weeks ago. Bailey wanted to lean forward, to get her first glimpse of the mysterious brother and his wife. But she refrained, holding back and letting Cal rise to greet them.

He stepped forward and the two brothers hugged for a long moment before the sister-in-law took her turn. When they moved closer, Bailey finally got a full view of them. Cameron was like a younger, shorter version of Cal, though he was well over six feet. His shoulders weren't as broad, but he had the same commanding presence and the same easy smile, the same dark hair and eyes. Cal was better looking, and she didn't think she was biased in thinking that. He was more classically handsome, debonair. He could have been a movie star in the forties. Or now, probably. The brother's looks were cuter, more boyish in nature. He stepped onto the porch and held out his hand to Bailey.

"Major."

"Lieutenant," she replied, greeting him with a hearty shake.

"My wife, Maggie," he said. "Fair warning: she's a hugger."

As if to prove the point, Maggie leaned forward and gave her a tight hug. "Hi, Bailey, it's so nice to meet you. We're big fans of Jane. And your dad."

"Me, too," Bailey said. "And it's so nice to meet you in return. I've heard him mention you. He said you're classy. That's a big deal in his view."

"Mine, too," Cam said, tossing his wife an affectionate wink.

Maggie turned to Cal and tapped the plastic container in her hands. "I brought cookies. Can I make a pot of coffee?"

"Absolutely," he said, easing his arm around her shoulders as he led her inside.

Cam and Bailey remained on the porch. "How's he doing?" Cam asked her.

She shook her head. "He's been quiet today. I think it's all bottle-necked in there."

"That sounds about right," Cam said. "Does he know what you have planned for tomorrow?"

"No, sir," she replied.

He grinned. "You know you outrank me, Major."

"Force of habit," she said.

"I know. What are we going to do about him when it's time?" he asked.

"I'll handle him."

"You know how?" he asked, tipping his head questioningly.

She shrugged, avoiding his gaze.

"Cam, can you bring in the coffee cake?" Maggie called from inside the house.

"Yes," he replied. "Maggie believes food cures everything," he explained to Bailey. "As soon as she got off the phone with you, she started baking."

"I'm inclined to agree with her," Bailey replied.

He picked up the bags at his feet. "Coming in?"

"You all need some family time. I'll stay out here, thank you," she said, settling back into the glider.

"If you change your mind, you're more than welcome," he said.

"Thank you," Bailey said.

He shouldered his bags and made his way inside.

Cal felt like a tenacious bandage had been ripped off everything internal. He was bruised, sore, shaken. The last thing he wanted to do was try and play host, to prop himself up and pretend everything was okay. And the easy, gentle adoration between Maggie and Cam was making it worse. What he really wanted was to go back onto the porch with Bailey, to hold her hand and stare silently into the warm, dark night.

"The place looks good," Cam said to try and cover the stilted, awkward silence.

"Thanks," Cal said, smiling slightly at Maggie as she set a mug of coffee and a plate of cookies before him. He reached for a cookie and then set it back down, standing. "I need some air, excuse me."

He stalked through the house, onto the porch, and kept going, suddenly claustrophobic and unable to breathe. Bailey stood and watched as he sprinted to the barn and took off. A second later, Cam bolted onto the porch.

"Which way did he go?" he asked.

"He took off on his horse."

Cam took a step as if to go after him, but Bailey stood. "I'll go, if you don't mind."

"No, I...okay." He remained rooted to the spot while she sped to the barn and tore out, barebacked. When he couldn't see her in the distance anymore, he turned and went back to the kitchen.

"Did you find him?" Maggie asked.

"Bailey went after him. That's kind of odd, don't you think?" He settled into a chair. Maggie slid into his lap, resting her head on his shoulder.

"She's in love with him."

"You saw her for thirty seconds. How could you possibly know that?"

"I have this thing called intuition," she said.

"That's kind of sad for her. There's no way Cal would…would he?" He rubbed her back. "Maggie?"

"I don't know, Cam. Something's off here, and I can't put my finger on it. Did he say anything to you about Bailey?"

"He said she's a friend, a good friend."

"If you described another woman that way, I'd cut her," Maggie said. "And then I'd cut you."

"Yeah, it pinged on my radar, but Cal would never cheat on Isabel. It's not in his makeup."

"I don't know," Maggie said, blowing out a breath.

"He wouldn't," Cam said, his tone defensive.

"I'm not arguing with you. I'm just trying to figure out what's going on. And I'm sad, so sad. I barely knew her, but it's still gut wrenching."

"I know. She and Cal got married when I was still in college, just a kid. I can't say she was ever the ideal sister-in-law, but she was still my sister-in-law."

"I know," Maggie said, cuddling up to him and kissing his cheek.

"Think I should go check on him?"

"How do you know where he went?" she asked.

"There's probably only one place he'd go."

"Give them a bit. It seems like he needs some space," Maggie said.

"Why? I'm his brother."

"If something happened to me, would you feel like talking the next day?"

He shuddered and drew her closer. "I never want to find out."

Cal was in the first place Bailey checked for him, at the watering hole where they'd gone swimming. She slid off her horse and sat down on the grass beside him.

"I felt like I couldn't breathe," he explained.

Bailey didn't comment. She sat silently by his side, offering unspoken comfort. After a few more minutes, he began to talk.

"You know what the worst part is? Behind all the horror, the grief, the shock, the anger, I feel relieved. My wife was murdered, and I feel relieved. What kind of man feels that way?"

"You can't control your feelings, Cal. They'll come, they'll go, they'll be horrible, they'll be wonderful. It has nothing to do with who you are. The only thing you can control is what you do with them and you were kind, gentle, caring. You tried to offer her a way out, a hand up. No one could have responded better in that situation or with more integrity. You have nothing to be ashamed about, absolutely nothing."

"Then why do I feel so bad?" he asked, beginning to cry again. Bailey put her arm around him and let him cry himself out. When his tears came to an end, he wiped his eyes.

"Thanks for being here, Bailey, for being a friend."

"I wouldn't be anywhere else," she said.

"Nothing like pity to bring people together, huh?" Cal said, swiping at his eyes once more.

"You think I pity you?" Bailey asked. She turned to face him.

"Don't you?" he asked. He finally looked at her, and it was as if the air between them came to a standstill and got sucked away. Now she was the one who couldn't breathe.

"Yes, I definitely do." She rested her left hand on his shoulder while her right hand brushed his cheek, wiping the last traces of his tears. "That first day I arrived, when you stepped out onto the porch, I thought, 'Now there's a man I'd like to pity. In fact, I don't ever think I've seen a man I'd like to pity more.' And then I got to know you, and understand the man you are, and the pity grew and grew until I'm so filled with pity I don't know what to do with myself. I have struggled under the weight of pity, half delirious with it." He smiled a little now. Her left hand let go of his shoulder and eased under his shirt, her palm pressing flat against his stomach. "These abs are the most pitiable part of you, I think."

"Bailey," he breathed, sucking a breath at her touch.

"Hold still and let me pity you proper," she said, leaning forward to press her lips to his. He reached for her to draw her closer. She leaned into him, practically lunging for him.

"Do you have any idea how long I..." he tried.

"Yes," she said, interrupting him with another kiss.

"How much I..."

"Yes," she said, interrupting him again.

"Dang, girl," he said.

She laughed and let go of his stomach to cradle his face in her hands, making it easier for her lips to reach him. He pulled her into his lap and kissed her in return the way she wanted, like he meant it for keeps. They paused a few minutes later, breathless and shaking. He rested his forehead on hers.

"I should have known you'd be the one to make the first move," he said.

"I think we both saw it coming a mile away," she said.

"I..." he began, but he wasn't able to complete that thought, either. A noise to his right alerted them of someone else's presence. They looked up to see his brother atop a horse, staring down at them with a mix of shock and disapproval.

Cam slid off his horse. Cal shot to his feet, Bailey toppling haphazardly to the ground. The two brothers faced off, neither saying a word. Bailey got to her feet slowly between them. Cam's eyes darted to her.

"It's not how it looks," Cal finally said.

"Really? Because how it looks to me is like your wife was murdered and you're making out with your head of security, the woman who's been living under your roof the last few weeks."

"Okay, I guess it is how it looks," Cal said.

"I should go," Bailey inserted, but he caught her hand.

"Stay, this concerns you too," he said. He took a breath. "Cam, there's a lot you don't know." He paused again and took another breath. "Isabel and I broke up a couple of years ago. She moved out, we've been living apart, been separated all that time. But even before that, things weren't good. Probably the last five years we've had issues, major, horrible issues between us."

"But she was at our wedding eighteen months ago and everything seemed fine," Cam said.

"I paid her twenty thousand dollars to come with me and pretend we were still okay."

"Why?" Cam breathed.

"I told myself it was because I didn't want to rain on your and Maggie's parade, to ruin your special day with sadness and bad news, to make myself the focus in any way. But the truth is I was too proud to let you know how badly I failed, and too ashamed to admit how far I'd sunk. I thought if I kept pretending everything was okay then everything would eventually be okay. But everything was very much not okay.

"We bickered over the ranch. Isabel threatened to take it. I used that as an excuse to hang on to an unhealthy relationship that ended ages ago. It felt like so much failure, too much. Then lately I learned Isabel got hooked on drugs. She took up with the head of the cartel."

"In other words her death has nothing to do with you or the ranch," Cam said.

"I think she probably made him mad, did something to turn him against her, and he thought it was a two birds with one stone situation. He'd get rid of her and use it to goad me," Cal said.

"How and where does Bailey factor into this?" Cam said. They were grown men, both in their thirties, but he had always looked up to Cal, ridiculously so, and he couldn't stand to have his idol tarnished so badly with the thought of an affair.

Cal paused and glanced at Bailey. "Bailey showed up, and I began to realize holding on to everything I needed to let go was causing everyone concerned a lot of harm. But I still couldn't seem to let it go. I just...I wanted everything to magically be okay. But I swear to you I didn't cheat on Isabel with Bailey, at least not physically. What you saw just now was a first. She's been a friend to me when I needed one and...more, at least in my heart, even if I didn't act on it." He looked at Bailey who gave him an encouraging smile in return.

"Do Mom and Dad know?" Cam asked.

Cal shook his head. "They stopped coming to the ranch a while ago because of Is and it was easier that way, easier to keep things quiet."

"I wish you had told me so I could have been here for you," Cam said.

"I do, too. And I'm sorry I kept it from you, sorry I've been so proud and secretive and stupid." He reached for his wedding ring, ripped it off his finger, and held it aloft, as if to hurl it.

Bailey caught his fist and pulled it back down. "You'll regret it."

He took a breath and shoved it in his pocket instead, nodding. They stood in silence a few minutes. "I don't know what to do now," Cal admitted.

"Maggie made a lot of sugary food," Cam volunteered. "According to her, it works like magic to make a body feel better."

"I could go for something sweet," Cal said. "How about you, little bit?" He slid his arm around Bailey.

"Definitely," she agreed.

"All right then." He put his other arm around Cam and gave his shoulders a squeeze.

"Did you guys both ride here bareback?" Cam asked, spying their horses.

"You've been gone a long time, city slicker," Cal said.

"I could still ride bareback," Cam boasted.

"Let's see it," Cal urged.

"I don't want to make Maggie worry."

"We won't tell," Cal promised.

"She has a way of sussing these things out," Cam said.

"Did you say sussing or sissy?" Cal asked.

"Can I take this opportunity to remind you the last time you prodded me to do something I broke my ankle, and it was at this very spot?" He pointed to the tree over the watering hole.

"You would have been fine if you hadn't stepped on that dead branch," Cal said, swinging up onto his horse.

"Regardless, I'm a grown man, not easily prodded into outdoing my big brother." He swung up onto his horse, too.

"I guess you're too old for a race back to the house," Cal said.

"Definitely," Cam agreed. "Last one there's a rotten egg." He took off like a shot, Cal close at his heels.

CHAPTER 20

The next day was slightly better. Grief and shock were still palpable, but now that the secrecy was over, Cal felt as if he could breathe, as if he could be himself and relax. He rose at his usual time and prepped the coffee.

Bailey walked in a minute later, her usually perky ponytail in place, her flawless clothes looking as if she'd ironed them when Cal knew for certain she hadn't. Someday he would ask her how she accomplished that.

"Morning," he said.

"Morning," she responded.

"Coffee's almost ready."

"Great. Would you like some oatmeal?"

"Yes, please."

She put the kettle on to boil and prepped their oatmeal.

"Coffee's done," he announced. "Black today?"

"Yes, please." The only changeable portion of her morning routine, as far as he'd been able to tell, was that sometimes she took her coffee black and sometimes she added cream and sugar. He didn't yet know what made the difference, and he added it to the list of things to ask her.

She reached to the counter beside him for her mug. He grasped her arm, pulled her close, and kissed her. She stood on her toes, leaning into him. When that still wasn't enough, he picked her up and backed her into the wall.

The tea kettle whistled, startling them apart.

"Thank you for letting me make the first move today," he said.

"Took you long enough," she replied, shaking out of his grasp to turn off the tea before it woke Maggie and Cam. She poured the boiling water over their oats and set the hot teakettle aside.

"Is it okay with you if I make the second move?" she asked.

"I'm going to have to insist on it," he said.

She drew him to her and kissed him. He picked her up and set her on the counter for easier reach. "Our oatmeal is going to get cold," she murmured a while later.

"This is where that microwave earns its keep," he replied.

But eventually he did lift her off the counter. They carried their oatmeal to the table. "How are you doing today?" she asked.

"Okay. It's hard. It would be hard any way she went, but like this…" he trailed off and shook his head.

"Have you thought about any arrangements?" she asked. She was set to leave on Friday, but maybe she could postpone. *No.* She was done foisting herself on him. She would only stay if he asked her to.

"Isabel hated stuff like that. We'll wait until the dust clears and have a celebration of life service in her hometown in California," he said. "I should call her parents."

"Did they know about the separation?"

"Yes. She blamed it all on me, and I'm fine with that, but I still owe them a call. It's only proper. I expect I'm going to get an earful. Isabel has never done any wrong in their eyes."

One didn't turn out like Isabel without reason. Bailey could only imagine what her parents were like. But she didn't say so. The woman was dead. There was no reason to bash her or flaunt her dislike.

Cal rested his hand on her knee. "You're pretty good at this comfort stuff."

"I only wish I could do more, could ease your suffering in some way."

"You've already done so much more than you could know. To tell you the truth, I was half afraid you'd go on some kind of vigilante revenge raid or something." He smiled at her. She stared at her coffee. "Bailey."

Finally she looked up. He scowled. "You're not planning something like that, are you?"

"I think the less you know, the better," she said.

"No, absolutely not, no. I forbid it."

"You forbid it?" she asked. She smiled, but it was more from irritation than amusement.

"That's right. I'm your boss, and I forbid it," he said.

"I'm leaving on Friday. Consider this my two days notice," she said.

"You can't." For a minute her heart leapt, believing he meant she couldn't leave. But no. "I will not allow you to go off half cocked on some kind of death mission with murderers and rapists."

"I have never gone off half cocked in my entire life. And I've kind of spent the last decade fighting murderers and rapists," she said, taking a sip of her coffee.

"Don't be casual when I'm trying to be angry and stern with you," he said, scowling.

"Don't be angry and stern with me when I'm busy picturing you shirtless," she said, earning a laugh from him.

"You stop that."

"Which part?"

"Which part do you think?" he asked.

"I don't know. Maybe you're shy and particularly modest," she said.

"I very much look forward to proving to you I'm not. But I can't do that if you're dead," he said.

"Better hurry. My plane leaves Friday."

He scowled at his oatmeal. "I haven't enjoyed this whole conversation."

"Not even the part where I pictured you shirtless which, by the way, still going on."

"Woman, you're making me flustered," he said.

"Am I?" she asked, imitating his soft southern twang as she gave his thigh a light squeeze.

"Is this what they teach in the marines these days?" he asked.

"Oh, no, baby, this is all natural," she said.

"To think what I've been missing out on all these weeks," he said, shaking his head.

"You still have a smidge of time," she said, leaning forward to kiss the little spot behind his ear.

"Girl, that's not nearly enough," he said. He cupped her chin with his hand and kissed her, but he didn't mention asking her to stay.

*L*ater that day, Maggie made supper and they invited Sully to eat with them. Sully and Cam had played football together when Sully was a freshman and Cam a senior and remained friends in the way only former teammates can.

"When are your parents coming back?" Sully asked the two brothers.

"Their cruise ends Saturday," Cam said.

"You didn't try to contact them to tell them?" Sully asked.

Cal shook his head. "There was nothing they could do. It's not like there's going to be a service, and they're pretty much stuck on the boat until Saturday. It seemed like it would needlessly upset them."

"Let's hope they don't get the news or TV," Cam said. Isabel's death had made national news, both because it was so gruesome and because she was a former Miss America, married to a former professional football player. Reporters had started to call almost immediately, but Bailey disconnected the landline. The remoteness of the ranch made it an unlikely spot for all but the most intrepid newshounds. So far none of those had shown up. As for Cal, his agent gave a statement on his behalf, and that seemed to stem the rising tide of curiosity seekers and ghouls.

They finished supper and pushed back from the table while

Maggie cut the pie she'd made that day. Bailey could see why his dad liked her so much. She was sweet and soft and domestic but also sharp and wickedly funny. She reminded Bailey a lot of her mom.

"I got some news today," Sully said, his tone grim. "They matched some DNA found on Isabel to Rodriguez, the head of the Cartel. It could only have been left by her killer, meaning he probably did it himself. There's a warrant out and a request for extradition, but you know how that goes. It's likely we'll never get him. I'm sorry, Cal. That's an extra blow, one I didn't want to have to deliver."

"It's about what I expected, Sully. It's not your fault," Cal said. Maggie set a piece of pie in front of him and squeezed his shoulders. He almost laughed at her unerring belief that food would make anything better. His mind flashed to a conversation Cam relayed to him when he and Maggie were engaged. They'd been in the middle of an argument when Maggie insisted on stopping to taste test their wedding cake. *You think cake can make everything better,* Cam had snapped. *Because it can. Cake can cure anything. Except diabetes,* Maggie had returned, making Cam laugh so hard he forgot what they were fighting about in the first place. He wanted a love like that. Bailey touched his knee, and he realized he had stared at his pie in silence for too long. So he stared at her instead, his heart filling with dreams and possibilities that by all rights should seem impossible at the moment.

"Someone needs to stop them," Sully said, drawing his attention back to the conversation. Except the conversation came to a standstill as everyone suddenly seemed unable to make eye contact with anyone else. "What?" Sully asked, as clueless as Cal, apparently.

"I think someone already has a plan to," Cal said, looking between Bailey and his brother. "You too, Cam?"

"Bailey made some good points on the phone," Cam said, scraping his fork across his empty plate.

"Look me in the eye and tell me you won't do it," Cal said. If his brother made the promise, he'd keep faith. He was that sort of man; they both were.

"Don't make him do that," Bailey said.

"You stay out of it. This is between me and him," Cal said, turning his anger on Bailey.

"No, it's not. This is war. That means it's between me and him." She motioned to Cam.

"Just stop. This is not Afghanistan," Cal said.

"No, it's not. You know why? Because there we had air and ground support. Here we have nothing. We're on our own, and it's only going to get worse," Bailey said.

"How much worse could it get than my wife's head in a box?" Cal roared.

"Next time it could be yours," Bailey said quietly before getting up and excusing herself from the table.

A minute later, Cal poured a glass of iced tea and quietly left the house. Bailey sat in the glider, rocking gently. He sat beside her and handed her the tea.

"No, thank you," she said.

He took a sip of the tea and set it on the table beside him. He slid his arm around her, and she leaned into him.

"I'm sorry I snapped at you," he said after a while.

"You're understandably upset about everything. I get it, and I don't blame you," she said. She didn't want to disturb the peace again, but she had to say what she needed to say. "Cal, you're going to have to trust me on this. They need to be stopped or it's going to keep going. Do you want Jinx to be next? Estralita?"

"I'm not saying they don't need to be stopped. I'm saying you don't need to be the one to stop them. That's what the law is for."

"When the law fails its people, the people take action. The government wasn't protecting you. Isn't that why you brought me here in the first place?"

"That was before," he said.

"Before what?" she asked.

"Before I fell in love with you," he said.

She paused. "I'm in love with you, too, Cal, but it doesn't change who I am or what I need to do."

"Bailey, I can't stand by and watch you put your life on the line for something that has nothing to do with you," he said.

She sat up and looked at him. "Nothing to do with me? It has everything to do with me. Haven't you been paying attention? I said I'm in love with you. Do you think that means I can let this go on, knowing what they're capable of, knowing what they've already done? And if you love me, it means accepting the soldier along with the woman. I will always be a marine, no matter where I am or what I'm doing. Semper Fi is more than an emblem on a jacket. This is what I signed up for; this is what I live for. If you have a problem with that, then you have a problem with me." She reached across him and shoved the glass of tea into his hands. He took a sip, not really thinking about it until she refused it, shoving it back into his hands with the words, "Drink up."

He froze. "Did you drug my tea?"

"Of course I didn't drug your tea."

But his head began to feel a little swimmy, exactly the same as when Jinx gave him the sedative two nights ago. "Then why won't you drink it?" he asked, still suspicious.

She took the tea, downed it, and tried to hand him the glass but his fingers felt too weak and thick to take it. "I don't feel so good," he murmured. Or at least he thought he did. The sound was tinny, hollow.

Bailey moved aside and helped him to lie down in the glider. She smoothed her hand over his head a few times. "Sleep, sir."

He grabbed her wrist. "You really didn't drug my tea?"

She shook her head. "I drugged your pie." She leaned in and kissed him full on the lips, and then everything faded to black.

CHAPTER 21

Sully and Cam stepped out onto the porch. "How long will he sleep?" Sully asked.

"A few hours at least. All night if we're lucky. Jinx should be here soon to keep an eye on him," Bailey said.

"I don't want to be you when he wakes up," Cam said, regarding his brother warily. He'd seen him in a temper enough times to know to be clear when he came to.

"Me neither," Bailey agreed. "But I'm leaving Friday."

"That's still on?" Sully asked.

"That's still on," Bailey said. "So I'll see you then. And, about tonight, you might want to turn your attention to the north, ignore any smoke or noises you hear from the south for a while. Just saying." She stood on her toes to kiss his cheek.

"Never a dull minute with you, girl," he said, giving her head an affectionate pat. "Cam, always good to see you."

"You too, Sul. Make your way to DC sometime, stop in for a visit."

"Might have to jog my way there to work off your pretty girl's cooking," he said, pressing his palm to his ridiculously flat stomach. "Goodbye, Maggie," he called through the door.

Maggie stepped out and gave him a hug. "It was so nice to see you again, Sully. Don't be a stranger."

"Same goes for you. There's always room for more in Texas," Sully replied.

"Someday, maybe," Cam said, slipping his arm around his wife.

They waved Sully away and then Cam and Bailey went to go change. Meanwhile Jinx arrived. Together he and Cam carried Cal to his room and tucked him into the big bed. A few minutes later, Cam and Bailey met back on the porch.

"About the plan," Cam began. "I think we're going to need something extra."

"What did you have in mind?" Bailey asked.

He checked his watch. "Your dad is sending us something from Lackland."

Her lip curled. "What could we possibly need from the air force?"

"A delivery vehicle," he said as a van made its way up the long lane. They watched as it stopped, the doors opened, and four men piled out, dressed in full gear and ready to go.

"This where you're from LT?" one of the men asked. "No wonder you're cranky. It's so hot the inside of my nose is sweating."

"Nice, Jones," Cam said. "Way to make a good impression. Beside him are Ethan, Shimmer, and Frog."

"Ugh, a jarhead," Jones said, surveying Bailey in her camo fatigues.

"That's Major Jarhead to you, sergeant," she replied.

"How can you tell I'm a sergeant when I'm not in uniform?" he asked.

She crooked her finger at him. He stepped closer, and she leaned in to whisper in his ear. "I can smell the inferior rank on you, princess."

He thumped his hand over his heart. "Hear that, boys? That's the sound of me in love."

"You're going to have to get in line behind my brother," Cam said.

"Where we at here, LT?" Shimmer asked.

"This is the Major's operation," Cam said, and the men's attention shifted to her.

Bless the military, she thought. It was the one place rank counted more than gender.

"Thank you, Lieutenant. Let me tell you what's going on." She summarized the situation and laid out their mission.

"Major, if I may interrupt," Cam said near the end. "I'd like to suggest adding a sniper for additional cover."

"That's an excellent suggestion, Lieutenant, but it leaves us a man short on the ground, unless you have a miracle up your sleeve," she replied.

"More like on the other side of the door. Maggie, you can come out."

Maggie stepped onto the porch with a sheepish smile. "I was only half eavesdropping, I promise. Stupid dishwasher kept drowning you out."

"I'm sorry, Maggie," Bailey apologized. "I didn't realize you'd be taking part in the operation or I would have invited you. I also didn't realize you'd served. What branch were you in?"

"The public library," Maggie said.

"She's a librarian. You'll get used to it," Cam promised as Bailey resisted the urge to stare. Maggie was so soft, so gentle, so feminine. She began to have more sympathetic understanding for people who couldn't believe she was lethal either.

"All right," she forced herself to turn away and stop staring speculatively at Maggie. "Excellent. Any questions?"

Jones raised his hand. "Are you married?"

"Any questions that don't make me lose immediate respect for you as a human and a soldier?" Bailey clarified.

"Oh, in that case no," Jones replied, lowering his hand.

"Well, then, gentlemen. Let's roll," Bailey said and they loaded up and headed out.

They left in two trucks. Cam drove one and Bailey drove the other. The four SEALs and Maggie sat in the back of Cam's truck. They would be depositing Maggie at a pre-chosen spot so she could set up her rifle.

"Are you going to take the kill shot this time, Maggie?" Jones asked. It had become something of a joke among them that, though Maggie was the best marksman any of them knew, she had never killed anyone.

"Oh, Jonesie, there are plenty of ways to disable a man without taking the kill shot, you know that," Maggie said, ruffling his hair. The truck stopped. Cam lifted her down and kissed her goodbye.

"Man, that woman is all kinds of sexy," Jones said, and Ethan mashed his palms over his ears.

"You gotta stop. That's my sister-in-law. I think my ears might actually be bleeding." He removed his hands from his ears and stared at them.

"You said the same thing the first time we met her," Jones reminded him.

"That was two years ago and, did I mention, she's now my *sister-in-law*," Ethan said. "By the way, Amelia and I are officially engaged. Save the date because you're all going to be in this one."

"When are you going to tell her parents you're already married to your fiancée?" Frog asked.

"We already did when we moved in together because they kind of freaked out," Ethan said. "The continued sham is for the sake of their distant family and friends. Or reasons. I don't know. At this point I'm beginning to think Amelia just wants the big wedding we didn't get last time around."

"Ah, young love," Shimmer said.

"When are you going to tell your parents?" Frog asked.

"Geez, I should probably call them, give them a heads up I'm seeing someone," Ethan mused.

Jones stared through the window at Bailey. "What is it with all the hot women in the world being near me but out of reach? What's the deal with her and LT's brother? Are they together, not together?"

"It doesn't matter anyway," Ethan said. "Don't you know who her dad is?"

"You?" Jones guessed.

"The Colonel," Shimmer supplied.

"What? I thought she was dating Blue."

"Different daughter."

"The Colonel replicated more than once? He really is like the terminator," Jones said.

"You know to this day no one's seen that cadet he made disappear," Frog said.

They stopped again when they reached the rendezvous point. They would ditch the trucks and walk the rest of the way, slipping over the border into Mexico by foot. They also split into two teams. The forward team—Bailey, Cam, and Frog—would be going in to draw fire and create a distraction while the second team—Ethan, Jones, and Shimmer—would be going in second to do what they needed to do. They were doubtless better trained than the cartel, but it would be a mistake to underestimate anyone who was armed with an agenda. The cartel had a lot of firepower. This they knew from Corrie's intel, though they would be doing recon to confirm.

They sneaked close for a look, using the thermal imager to get a look at how many bodies were inside the house. They counted six bodies all sitting around a table. Since it was nearly the middle of the night, Bailey imagined they were playing cards or counting something.

"How good is your intel?" Cam asked.

"Three fingers worth," Bailey replied.

"What?"

"It's good." It hadn't taken long to break Corrie, and then he sang like a little bird, giving her names, locations, and details on what was in the house and who was in charge. He had told her the name Rodriguez before Sully did.

"First team, who wants to take point?" she asked. The military was a special breed in that, when asked which of them wanted to shoot a gun while running toward a heavily armed compound, there could often be a squabble about who got to do it.

"I'll go," Cam volunteered. "I never get to do the fun stuff anymore. Do you want to call it?"

"It's your ball, Lieutenant," Bailey said.

He stood. "Maggie is so not going to like this," he said before holding his gun aloft and taking off at a sprint toward the house.

When he was close enough to be heard but still too far away to inflict casualties, he began to spray the ground around the house with bullets.

There was an almost comic scrambling from inside the house as men dove for guns and ammo before running outside to give chase.

"Frog, we're up," Bailey said. "Second team, looks like your target is clear." She and Frog jumped into the fray, diverting the gunfire in two separate directions to keep things chaotic. The cartel had no idea where or who they were shooting, nor which direction it came from. It was almost like a child's game of tag, except with heavy-duty automatic weaponry.

It was supposed to be random; the darkness should have provided cover. But the moon slipped from behind a cloud and Bailey caught a glimpse of Rodriguez. He was their secondary target, and she couldn't help but give chase. Her legs pumped hard with the effort it took to keep up with him. He was large, in good shape, and she was weighted down by pounds of armor, weaponry, and ammo. There came a point when she thought she had the drop on him, but he turned at the last moment, his gun pointed directly at her face. Bailey's gun was in his face, too, and they stood still, taking stock of each other from three feet apart.

"Question," she said. "If you have a Mexican standoff in Mexico, is it just a standoff?"

He didn't answer. She tsk'd. "No sense of humor? Prison's not going to go well for you."

"I'm not going to prison," he said.

"Are you asking me to kill you? Because I will," she promised.

"How about I kill you instead?" he said, smiling.

"You're taking an awfully big chance you're faster on the trigger than I am. You piddle with that little gun and probably do okay, but I'm a marine marksman. I guarantee if I go, you're going with me," she said. "And my friends are just about done and will be along any minute."

"So will mine," he said.

She shook her head. "You hear that? That silence? The shooting stopped because it's over. We flushed you out to round you up."

His gaze flickered, but he also tightened his grip on the gun.

"I have a good idea, one I think we'll find mutually agreeable. I have a suggestion for how we can both lower our weapons without taking a shot," she said. "Here's what we do. I am slowly going to take a step about a foot to the right, and then I'm going to lower my gun. I highly suggest you do the same."

"Why would I do that?" he asked.

"It's the honorable thing to do," she said, easing slightly to her right as she had said. She lowered her gun. He grinned and braced his feet to take his shot, but before he could pull the trigger his right shoulder exploded with a bullet from Maggie's gun. He screamed, his gun clattering uselessly to the ground. Bailey picked it up. "On your knees," she commanded. He sank to his knees, more than likely because he was in too much pain to support himself than because he was being compliant, a fact demonstrated when he lunged for her legs, intending to take her down. Instead she kicked his wounded shoulder, hard, and aimed her gun at his head.

"Give me a reason," she said. And then she realized she already had a reason. She remembered Cal's scream the night he found Isabel. He would have to live with the pain of that moment for the rest of his life, all because the animal before her hacked a woman to death and presented her to her husband as a prize. She could end this now. She could save everyone time, effort, and money by getting rid of the piece of human waste before her.

"Bailey," Cam called, but not until he yelled, "Major Dunbar," did she snap to attention and lower her weapon.

"This is not over. You think it ends with me? It doesn't," Rodriguez hissed through teeth gritted with pain.

"I wouldn't be so sure about that," Bailey said. "Ethan, how are we doing on the clock?"

Ethan checked his watch. "Let's see here. 5, 4, 3, cover your ears now." They covered their ears as the house a couple hundred yards away exploded, completely wiped off the map in a spray of fine powder.

"Oh, uh-oh. Was that your house?" Bailey taunted the man on the ground. "The one where you had all your drugs and guns and money? Oopsie. Well, no matter. The good news is I've dealt with your suppliers in Afghanistan, and they're really sweet and understanding. I'm sure if you simply explain...Oh, wait a minute, no. They're going to kill you. Bummer."

Cam moved closer and inspected the man's shoulder. "Maggie do that?"

"Your girl can shoot," Bailey said. She turned over her shoulder and mouthed Maggie a "thank you" with a little wave. In response, Maggie flickered a light. She turned back to the SEAL team and their prisoners. "If you men would take this refuse back to the truck, I'll join you in a minute. I have one more little thing to do." She grasped Rodriguez by the hair, pulled his head back, and used her phone to snap a photo. Then she pulled out a handheld device and printed the photo.

When that was done, she ran down the road and tapped on a door. Estralita answered, looking petrified. "It's Bailey," she said in Spanish, in case the older woman was too scared to summon her impressive translation skills. "Can I talk to your grandson?"

Estralita yelled for Hector, her grandson. He appeared, looking as scared and uncertain as his grandmother had. Bailey handed him the picture. "I want you to show this to everyone you see tomorrow and pass along a message for me. Tell them if the cartels pass over *Señor* Ridge's land again we'll come for them, and I'll personally do worse than I did to Rodriguez. Can you do that for me?" He was a reliable, chatty boy of fourteen who would have no trouble relating the night's tale to everyone he encountered.

"*Si*," he replied, nodding enthusiastically as he stared at the picture. "*Senorita*, are you playing football on Sunday?"

"Not this Sunday," she said.

"Next time, can I be on your team?" he asked, his face eager.

"Absolutely," she called. She ran back down the road, tossing him a wave over her shoulder.

CHAPTER 22

That night the local jail received six anonymous prisoner donations, dumped on the doorstep with a note that read, "Please take care of our boys. We can no longer care for them as they need to be cared for. The big one likes to be punched regularly. Sincerely, a loving mom."

The atmosphere was festive on the drive back to the ranch. It was over, and things couldn't have gone better. And then they arrived back at the house and saw Cal standing on the steps, arms crossed over his chest. The party atmosphere faded and died and they trooped silently from the trucks.

He regarded them with a glare a moment before speaking. "Ethan, Frog, Shimmer, Jones." They had only met once at Maggie and Cam's wedding. He hadn't seemed to be paying attention to their names, but apparently he had taken note.

"Did anyone else just pee their pants a little?" Jones whispered, causing the others to snort a muffled laugh.

"There's Maggie's pie and cake and cookies left, if y'all would like to go in and have some." His eyes narrowed on Cam. "I'll deal with you later. You stay," he added to Bailey.

Bailey remained where she was, at the base of the stairs. Everyone else filed silently into the house.

"I take it things went well," he said.

"Yes. Rodriguez is…"

He pressed his hands to his ears and shook his head. "I don't want to hear it."

She ran lightly up the steps, stopping on the step above him to give her a better height advantage, and peeled his hands from his ears. "Incarcerated," she said loudly enough to be heard.

He blinked at her. "Oh."

"You thought I went there to kill him in cold blood?" she guessed.

"Yes."

"I can't say I didn't think about it. But that wasn't the purpose of the mission."

"Are you okay?"

"Yes, are you?"

"I'm groggy," he said.

"Oh, right. Sorry about that."

"I'm mad at you," he informed her.

"You should be," she agreed.

"You drugged me, you defied my wishes, and even wearing camo and grease paint you're incredibly hot." He picked her up.

She secured her arms around his neck, her legs around his waist. "That makes you mad?"

"No, it makes me mad I'm trying to yell at you but the hotness factor keeps getting in the way."

"How do you think I made it through boot camp?" she asked. "What can I do to help you be un-mad at me?"

"I'm going to have to ponder on it a bit. In the meantime, I guess you'll have to kiss me," he said and kissed her.

Inside everyone stood at the window, eating sweets and blatantly watching Bailey and Cal. "I hope that's not how he's going to deal with the rest of us," Jones said.

"Nah, he'd be hard pressed to pick you up, Jones," Ethan said, smacking him in the gut.

"It's all muscle," Jones replied.

"Muscle jiggles now?" Shimmer interjected.

"Those are power vibrations," Jones said. "I can't help it my mom's a good cook."

"You could if you moved out of her basement," Cam added.

"Jokes on you, LT, my mom kicked me out of her basement," Jones said.

"You can live in our basement, Jonesie," Maggie offered.

"Thanks, Maggie," he said, giving her a one-armed hug around the neck.

"Who's going to tell him they don't have a basement?" Ethan stage whispered, and everyone snickered.

When the pie was finished, they frittered to bed to catch a few hours of sleep before they flew back home. Cam and Maggie curled up on the couch.

"I love it here," she declared.

"I'm glad," he said, pulling her into his lap and tucking her close. "Think you could live here fulltime?"

She paused. "I don't know. As much as I enjoy it, it wouldn't be an easy transition. And we'd have to leave Amelia and Ethan and Blue and Jane and The Colonel and all our other friends."

"But we'd be here with Cal and, I'm assuming, Bailey. And then we'd still get to see The Colonel," he pointed out.

She shifted to see him better. "Are you ready to leave your job?"

"No, but I have three years until my trust matures, and then I'm going to have to decide if I'm going to sell out to Cal or keep my part of the ranch. And I'm honestly not sure what to do."

"A lot can happen in three years."

"I'll say," he said, giving her a squeeze. Three years ago he didn't even know her, a fact that was unbelievable to him now. What was life like before Maggie? He had no idea. All he could remember was a big gray blob. He'd grown up on a ranch, gone to a prestigious university, been a decorated Navy SEAL, become a spy, and yet it felt like his life hadn't started until he began sharing it with her.

"We haven't stayed up all night in forever," she said.

"I don't think we're going to make it now," he said.

"It's only two hours until sunrise," she said.

"Baby, you're going to be asleep before this conversation ends," he said.

"No way, I can make it," she said, yawning.

"That's right, there's no way you can make it," he said, and she laughed. The sound of her laughter made him smile and he held her a little tighter.

"Did I tell you I love you today?" she asked.

"Yes."

"Did I tell you you're in big trouble for taking point on the mission?"

"Yes."

"Pretty sure not."

"I knew you had me covered," he said.

"You're such a handsome liar. It's confusing to my senses." Now it was his turn to laugh while she smiled. "What do you think they're doing out there?"

"If I had to guess, I'd say making out," he said.

"Again?"

"Don't you remember how we were in the beginning? When we couldn't get enough of each other, when we couldn't keep our hands to ourselves."

"We're like that now," she reminded him.

"Ain't life grand?" he asked, but she didn't answer. In the time it took him to speak the words, she fell asleep.

On the porch, Bailey and Cal were arranged in a remarkably similar position, only they sat on the glider and his long legs rocked them gently back and forth.

"I should go wash my face," she said without making any sort of move to leave.

"I think we've already established my deep interest in the grease paint," he said.

"It's a tad disturbing to me how vested you seem in canoodling a commando," she said.

"I only like the ones with long hair and smoking hot bodies," he said.

"You've described half the commandos I know," she said. "Do you think we'll make it until sunrise?"

"I know I will, thanks to my sedative-induced eight hour nap," he said.

"You sound a little bitter for someone so well rested," she said, and he gave her a squeeze. She took his hand and studied it, letting her fingers smooth over the callouses. She touched her callouses to his. "We're bump buddies."

"We're hard working buddies," he said. "I've never met a girl who can keep pace with branding for the entire day. The men were floored. I think they were taking bets on how soon you'd conk out."

"I know. I bet I'd stay in the whole day. Won fifty bucks," she said. "Always bet on yourself. That's my motto."

"You have a lot of mottos. I'm losing track," he said.

"I'll diagram them for you," she said.

They watched the sun come up that way, bantering, talking about nothing. There was no mention of the fact that Bailey was scheduled to leave in a few hours, nor any mention of their relationship—present or future—beyond the mutual admission of feelings for each other.

Inside the SEAL team members began to stir. Bailey slipped away to take a shower while Cal and Maggie made breakfast. Maggie was the only non-military, non-cowboy in the room and therefore the only non-morning person. It was amusing to all of them to watch the usually perky and cheerful woman stumble around dazed and cranky, and they hounded her relentlessly for it.

"Quick, Maggie, what's four plus seven?" Frog demanded.

"Coffee," Maggie muttered.

"What's the square root of nine?" Shimmer asked.

"I'm going to stop you right there. The answer to everything is coffee," Maggie said.

"Who do you love the most?" Ethan tried.

She paused. "Cam, in a big field of coffee." She sat and rested her head on the table while Cam rubbed her back and the other men in the group tried to goad her into further conversation.

"There's something seriously wrong with all of you," she mumbled, the sound muffled by her arm.

They ate together, sharing the familial sense of accomplishment only a successful mission can bring. Then they said goodbye. The SEAL team members returned to Lackland, ghosting away with no traces as if they'd never been there at all. Cam and Maggie were staying another day. They said goodbye to Bailey and made themselves scarce.

Sully would arrive soon. Cal needed to address the issues between them, but he kept putting it off.

"Your hair is down today," he noted. "It's the only time since you've been here, except for the dance." They stood on the porch in each other's embrace. His fingers sifted gently through her tresses.

"I'm not working today," she explained.

"Why do you take your coffee black some days and others not?" he asked.

She gave him an enigmatic smile. "I'm going to leave you to puzzle over that one."

"You understand that I want you here," he said when he could put off the inevitable conversation no longer.

But Bailey understood nothing. How could he let her go with what was between them? Unless what was between them wasn't what she thought. It was that possibility that held her back and kept her silent.

"It's been a rough week, a rough couple of years, a rough decade. I feel like I need to get myself together," he said.

"I understand. But you need to understand I'm not the kind of woman who waits around."

"What's that supposed to mean?" he asked.

"I've been using Jinx's mom's blood pressure cuff to keep track of myself while I'm here. Every day my numbers have been perfect. If I can get clearance from a doctor, I can re-up my commission. If and when that happens, I can't guarantee where I'll be in a week, a month, a year. Surprisingly, the marines don't much care about my love life."

"Did it occur to you the reason your blood pressure is down is because you're here and if you go back it's going to go back up?"

"Yes, but now I know all I have to do to fix it is to spend a couple of weeks in the country. So I'll actually use my vacation time and get away somewhere. Problem solved."

She was frustrating him with her stubbornness, but he didn't say so. Spending fifty weeks of the year on a job that brought her to death's door was no way to live, in his opinion. But as he wasn't able to offer her an alternative, he had no say in the matter.

"Sully's going to be here soon," she said and stood on her toes to kiss him. "Definitely going to miss those lips," she added when the kiss was over. They'd had so little time to explore what was brewing between them.

"I do love you, Bailey. You know that," he said.

"I think I do," she replied, and he frowned. Did she not understand this was something he had to do? His wife of a decade was murdered mere days ago. It wasn't the right time to start a new relationship. If only she would stay a while longer, give him more time…

Sully's car turned up the long lane. They turned to face him, arm in arm.

"Y'all look like we're about to play Red Rover," Sully announced as he stepped form his truck. "You still going today?"

"Sure enough," Bailey said, imitating his gentle twang.

"Well all right then. Say your goodbyes."

"We already did," Bailey said. She shouldered her duffle and stepped away from Cal. It would do no good to prolong the moment. They had said all they would allow themselves to say. She hopped up into the truck, without assistance this time, and faced forward, not allowing herself to look back as the truck wound its way back down the long lane.

CHAPTER 23

Cal wandered back into the kitchen where Cam and Maggie stood talking and laughing. Maggie had finally woken all the way and was back to her cheerful self.

"There's one piece of bacon left," she announced. "I'll arm wrestle you for it."

"She cheats," Cam whispered in a loud aside.

"Everybody cheats for bacon," she returned.

"I'm good, you can have it," Cal said. He sat, feeling sore and tired for no reason he could figure.

"Did Bailey get off okay?" Cam asked, his tone bordering on tentative.

"Yep." Cal drummed his fingers on the table and stood. "Think I'll go for a ride."

"What is it with you cowboys?" Maggie asked after he'd gone. "Every time one of you gets upset you go off on a horse somewhere?"

"Pretty much," Cam agreed.

"If we had horses, we'd never finish an argument," she said.

"Now you know why my parents have been happily married for forty years," he said. He lifted her onto the counter, resting his hands on her hips. "It would seem we have the house to ourselves. What to do, what to do?"

"We're getting low on pie," Maggie said.

"Woman, we have this big place to ourselves for an hour, and you want to bake?"

"Pie takes an hour in the oven. If we hurry, we'll have all that time together to find something to do. And then after, there will be pie. Doesn't that sound nice?" she asked, slipping her arms around his neck.

"I'll peel the apples, you make the crust," he said.

"You are the master of foreplay, Cameron Ridge."

"Let's hurry up so I can go for my doctorate," he said, and she laughed.

When Cal returned a while later, he saw them frantically assembling a pie.

"Y'all enter a contest or something?" he asked.

"No, we enjoy speed baking together," Maggie hedged. "It's a sport in my family."

"Is that a thing?" Cal asked.

"Yes, it goes hand in hand with a sport where your wife makes promises that never come true," Cam said. He sank into a chair at the table beside his brother. "Cal, we need to talk."

"I don't want to talk about anything," Cal said.

"You mean you don't want to deal with anything," Cam returned.

"Wait, let me try. I'm getting pretty good at knowing how to handle Ridge men." Maggie dusted her hands and went to stand beside Cal. She rested her hand on his shoulder. "Cal, your self-immolating behavior, while noble, is not conducive to achieving the desired outcome. It's a negative interpretation of what should be a positive encounter."

Cal blinked at her and leaned around her to look at his brother. "What's the non-librarian translation of that?"

"You think you're being a hero by pushing Bailey away, but instead you're being a tool. Go get your girl."

Cal pushed away from the table and stood up. "All right then."

Maggie beamed at his retreating backside. "See? I totally fixed it."

"What's it like in your world, pretty girl?" Cam asked, tilting his head at her.

"There are fifty minutes left on the pie clock. I could show you, if you like," she offered.

"Well, I'm not going to say no to that."

She stood and prepared to dart away. "I'll race you."

"I have a better idea." He picked her up, tossed her over his shoulder, and carried her to their room.

*ailey was stuck in the middle seat. She craned her neck, trying to see over the man to her right—who was already asleep—to say a final goodbye to Texas. The seat to her left creaked. She turned to see a man wearing a familiar looking jersey. She had seen a similar one hanging in Cal's den.

"Who's on your shirt?" she asked.

The man turned his back to her so she could read the name. "Calhoun Ridge," he said at the same time she read the words.

"Are you a big fan?" she asked.

"Oh, yeah, that guy could have been a legend."

"He *is* a legend," Bailey said, her heart squeezing painfully.

"Yeah, he was pretty amazing, and then he walked away, just like that." He snapped his fingers. "You know his family ranch is somewhere around here. He's like a total recluse now. And his wife was murdered, so it seemed like a good time to pull the shirt back out. Solidarity, you know? Man, he shoulda stayed in the NFL."

"He wouldn't have been happy there. The ranch is his life."

"Doesn't make sense to me."

"It wouldn't to most men," she said.

"You're a fan, too, I take it?" he asked.

"The biggest," she said, smiling. Her smile must have been a bit too enthusiastic because the guy leaned toward her, resting his elbow on the armrest between them.

"Where you headed?"

Before Bailey could answer, a shadow fell on them. "Excuse me, would you mind trading seats with me?" Calhoun towered over them.

The guy glanced up with a scowl. "Get your own seat."

"I have one, but I wondered if you'd like to trade. I kind of need to talk to her."

"No way. This is the seat I paid for, and this is where I'm going to stay," the man said.

"I'll give you a hundred bucks," Cal offered.

The guy shook his head.

"How about his autograph?" Bailey interjected, and the guy did a double take.

"Geez, are you really him?"

"Depends on who you mean," Cal said. He pulled out a piece of paper, scribbled his autograph, and handed it to the guy. The guy held it to his face like Charlie when he won the Golden Ticket. "Uh, guy, the chair?"

"What? Oh, right, right. Sorry. Good luck." He traded spots with Cal and gave him the double thumbs up.

Cal returned it. "Maybe I should have let him stay. It looked like you guys had a good thing going."

"Eventually things would have become awkward. Turns out we both love the same guy. What are you doing here, Cal? You do realize you're on an airplane that's about to fly. In the air. Off the ground."

"I didn't make it in time to stop you before you got on, and it was the only way they'd let me through. You know, the FAA is kind of a buzz kill when it comes to true love."

"It's almost like terrorism is their main concern in life. Tunnel vision much?" she said. "Also, at what point in this flight are you going to tell me what you're doing here?"

"I..." he began but then the flight attendant stood to give the pre-flight spiel. Bailey tuned it out, but Cal focused on it like there was going to be an exam later. Finally the talk was over.

"You were saying," Bailey said.

"Sir, your seatbelt," the flight attendant interrupted. Cal jumped to attention and buckled his belt, testing it twice to make certain it was secure.

"I think you're good," Bailey told him.

"Right. You left, and the house was…" His attention drifted out the window as the plane began to roll. "We're moving now."

"It was bound to happen eventually," she said, squeezing his arm. "The suspense is sort of killing me here."

"I'm sorry," he said, drawing his attention from the window to her. "Bailey, I thought I would let you go for a bit, to heal, to get myself together. And then I would present myself to you, whole and healthy. But I realized…" the airplane had finished taxiing and began to pick up speed. Cal reached for his airsick bag and bent forward, closing his eyes.

Bailey rubbed his back soothingly. He breathed into the bag a few times and faced her. "I realized I'm already whole, and you're the reason why. You've brought me back to health, back to living. Without you there I…"

The plane began to accelerate and he pressed the bag back to his face, breathing hard and squeezing her hand.

He lowered the bag and blurted a quick stream of words. "Without you there, I'm half a person, half a heart again. I need you with me, and I want you with me. I love you." He closed his eyes and pressed the bag to his mouth again, taking a few puffs. The plane began its ascent and his face drained of color.

Bailey peeled the bag out of his fingers, turned him to face her, and kissed him, sliding her fingers across his scalp so when he reached out it was for her and not the bag. Once they were safely in the air and the bumps and jostles of ascension were over, she pulled back a bit. "Yes. I realize you haven't actually asked me anything, but I'm saying yes preemptively because I'll say yes to whatever you want of me for the rest of our lives. Yes to you, yes to babies, yes to the ranch, yes to Texas, yes to anything you suggest. If you want to sell the ranch, move to Siberia, and become ice mongers, I'll say yes to that too."

"I don't think ice monger is a thing, but let's go back to the part about the babies. Exactly how soon can I get you pregnant, and is there enough time to make an honest woman of you first?"

"That depends."

"On what?" his said, his tone wary.

"On whether or not Estralita can make enough stew and corn-bread for a crowd."

"She has, she can, and she will," Cal promised.

"Then two weeks ought to do it."

"Do you really want to get married at the ranch?" he asked.

"Yes, I've always wanted to get married at home," she said. He reached for her, but she put up a hand. "Are you sure you don't want to save that for the landing?"

"We're floating through the sky in a metal death box. We're not guaranteed a landing," he said.

"Good thing you're not about to marry a pilot," she said.

"We all have our crosses to bear. Mine is that the woman I'm in love with hates gravity. You know when I get you good and pregnant, you're going to have to keep both feet on the ground."

"We'll talk," she promised.

"It's non-negotiable," he said.

"Yes, sir," she said.

"Are you doing the thing where you pretend to agree with me but in reality you're going to keep doing exactly what you want to do?" he asked.

"Yes, sir," she said.

"You're going to make me crazy, aren't you?" he said.

"For the rest of our lives."

"Promise?"

"You have the word of a marine."

"Remind me what that's worth again."

"Everything," she said.

"I believe it completely," he said and kissed her again.

EPILOGUE

The first time Calhoun Ridge got married, it was in St. Patrick's Cathedral in New York City. He and Isabel each had eight attendants and a total of five hundred guests. The pictures of their wedding made *People* magazine, and Isabel was on a pre-wedding reality show for rich bridezillas.

The second time Calhoun was married, it was in the barn of his ranch with a few chairs and lights hastily assembled. His brother stood up for him, and Bailey's sister Jane stood up for her. There were less than fifty people in attendance. His housekeeper made a spicy stew and cornbread. Sully's mother, an amateur photographer, took a few photos for free, and any reporters who might have tried to show up would have been tossed out on their heads.

Bailey's dad gave her away, wearing his full and impressive uniform, the entire front of which was weighted down by medals and pins. Bailey wore a simple white satin dress, a sharp contrast to the massive beaded monstrosity Isabel wore a decade a go, one with a train so long it rivaled Princess Diana's. It was hard not to make comparisons between that day and this one, and it was hard not to feel grateful, ridiculously so, over the second chance he'd been given. Bailey was the kind of woman he should have looked for in the first place, a woman who valued hard work and personal integrity as much as he did. Those things might not be glamorous or sexy or end up on the cover of a magazine. But they were better indicators of happiness and fulfillment and he loved her, adored her, really. There was something extra special about knowing she reserved her soft side for him, his *diabla loca*.

After the wedding and the meal and the cake, they cleared the floor and danced. Cal enjoyed himself, enjoyed being with his family and friends, but he also longed to get away, to have Bailey all to himself, to begin their lives. His plan was to ease her out, to edge her toward an exit and steal away with her. But Bailey, it turned out, was not as into the plan as he was.

"My family is here. What are they going to think when I disappear?" she whispered. They were near the door, beneath the hayloft, as Cal attempted to urge her away.

"That you're ready to start your honeymoon with your ridiculously eager husband," he said.

"Give me one more hour," she said, pressing her palm to his cheek.

"Okay, but that's one less hour I have to get you good and pregnant," Cal said.

"Are you really sure you want to have a baby this soon?" she asked. She didn't have a ton of female friends, but the ones she did have always seemed to lament the fact their husbands didn't want kids as soon as they did.

"I have never been more sure about anything, present company excluded. I want us to have kids, a lot of kids, and very soon."

"Yes, I am so down with that plan," Maggie said, poking her head over the side of the hayloft. There were pieces of hay stuck haphazardly all over her head. "You guys should have kids stat."

"Girl, get down from there. Do you know what you look like you've been doing?" Cal exclaimed.

Cam's head appeared beside hers. "What's she look like she's been doing?"

"Probably exactly what she's been doing," Cal said.

"We were playing with the kittens," Maggie said, holding a kitten aloft. "Mostly."

Cam dropped his head to his hand. "Maggie, why did you add that 'mostly'? We were in the clear until then."

"Not really," Bailey said. "We're going back to the party. You kids have fun."

"We really were playing with the kittens," Maggie called.

"Mostly," Cam added. He sat back and set aside his kitten, reaching for her instead. "You know, if they're having a baby, we should really consider."

"Are you saying that because you want to have a baby or because you want to beat your brother?"

"Competition makes the world go round," he said, his hand smoothing up and down her arm. He started picking pieces of hay from her hair and then gave up when he realized there were too many. She was ridiculously lovely, and he couldn't get over the fact that she was his forever.

"I think we're going to be okay here," Maggie told him, easing her palms on his chest.

"How? If they get pregnant tonight, they'll have a baby first."

"Trust me, we're going to be okay," Maggie said.

"That only works if we…" he froze. "Maggie, are you trying to tell me you're pregnant?"

"A little bit," she said.

There was an exclamation from the hayloft and everyone turned to look.

"You know what I bet's going on?" Cal asked.

"Thanks to that eighth grade biology class, I think I do," Bailey answered.

"I bet because they heard us talking about having a baby, they're planning to have a baby now, too. Cam's competitive like that. I have no idea where gets it," Cal said.

"What?" Bailey exclaimed. "She's younger than I am, and he's way, *way* younger than you."

"One 'way' would have been plenty sufficient, thank you."

"We'll see about that," she said and, taking his hand, led him over to her family. "Mom, Dad, I think we're going to take off. It's been a long day and we're exhausted. Thank you for being here. I love you so much." She hugged them and turned to her sisters and her sister's boyfriend. "Poppy, Jane, Blue. Much love, safe travels." Cal said his goodbyes, shook hands all around, and then they were done.

"One of us seems like a cow being rushed to slaughter on a conveyer belt, and I'm not sure if it's us or them," Blue said as Bailey and Cal dashed away.

"Something's got her dander up, but I can't imagine what," The Colonel said.

"Someone probably said *Rambo* Two was better than *Rambo* One and now Bailey has to beat them into submission," Jane suggested.

"Jane, don't joke about things like that," The Colonel snapped, his eyes narrowed. "*Rambo* One was a masterpiece, never to be outdone."

"You're a man of many layers, sir," Blue noted.

Meanwhile, Cal and Bailey reached the hayloft. "Hey," Bailey called, pausing until Maggie and Ridge popped their heads up. She pointed to her eyes, then their eyes, then her eyes again and she and Cal left the barn.

"What was that about?" Maggie wondered.

"They're onto us," Cam said.

"You think they know I'm pregnant?"

"No. If they knew that, they'd probably go steal a five month old to make good and certain they got the first baby. They're trying to beat us, but they have no idea we've already won," he said, rubbing his hands together in triumph.

"I'm not sure this family can handle another military personality," Maggie said.

"Too late now," Cam replied.

"One of the four of us is going to have to be the voice of reason," Maggie said. "My money's on Cal."

"What are we going to do about work?" Cam asked.

"We're going to let me keep working for as long as I can, and then we'll figure it out."

"But…"

She pressed a finger to his lips. "Sweetheart, we can't preplan every minute of our lives."

"We can try."

"Then we would miss out on the little surprises, like this pregnancy."

"You're good for me in all the ways," he said, his hand smoothing the flyaway hairs from her face.

"You don't get to pretend to be the lucky one in this scenario. I sat in my library eating a muffin when you plucked me out of obscurity and changed my world."

"Best day ever," he said. "Except all the ones that came after, up to and including this one."

"When do you think we should tell Bailey and Cal their efforts to beat us to the punch are futile?" she asked.

"Let's give them a couple of months of futility first. They'll thank us later," he said.

"Did I tell you I love you today?" she asked.

"Yes."

"Did I tell you twins run in my family?"

He froze. "No."

"You're thinking your brother would never be able to compete with twins, huh?" she asked.

"A little bit, yeah."

"You have a sickness."

"Lucky for me I also have the cure," he said and pulled her close for a kiss.

Thank you for reading *The Soldier and the Cowboy,* the fourth book in the Spies Like Us series. For further reading, please check out my website at www.vanessagraybartal.com

ABOUT THE AUTHOR

Vanessa Gray Bartal is a foodie who spends her time trolling bakeries and dreaming of new ways to use sourdough. When she is not baking (or eating), she loves to make music and spend time with her husband, three children, and sheepadoodle in rural Ohio. Her dream is to fill her books with enough coziness and warmth to brighten someone's day and make them smile. She would love to hear from you on Facebook or through email.